Desmond sat Ivy gently on the bed, then caressed her face. "You're beautiful."

"Because of you. The stylists..."

He shushed her with a finger to her lips. "Not that. You. Naturally."

Without breaking eye contact, he reached for one of her designer-clad feet and slipped off a shoe. He placed a thumb in the arch of her foot and massaged it in gentle circles. He removed the other shoe, then pulled her up and turned her around. "Are you sure?"

In answer, Ivy reached up in an attempt to unzip her own dress.

Desmond chuckled softly, sexily, kissing each spot revealed as the zipper slid down. He eased the silky material off her shoulders, caressing her from behind.

Could she handle him? Could she in all honesty handle any of this?

She didn't know, but she was about to find out.

* * *

The Nanny Game by Zuri Day
is part of The Eddington Heirs series.

Dear Reader,

Meet the Eddington Heirs. Desmond Eddington is the oldest son of Derrick and Mona, and the official ringleader of his brother, Jake, and sisters, Maeve and Reign. I had a wonderful time making their acquaintance and can't wait for you to get to know them! Together, they head up Eddington Enterprise, a family-owned financial services conglomerate that reaches around the globe. That's where we meet Desmond—ready to cut loose on the weekend after a hard week's work. But life has other plans. And that's where Ivy comes in.

There are so many things I loved about writing this story. One was developing the undeniable yet opposing chemistry between Desmond and his heroine, the powerful ego and the quiet strength. The other was creating and expanding Point du Sable, the fictitious township outside Chicago. I've learned that being the developer/architect/mayor/counsel of entire municipalities is one of my favorite things to do! The power of being able to create what I want, how I want. Remembering that in real life the same is true. I, we, have the power to create the lives we desire. Just as you'll see Desmond and Ivy do while playing the nanny game.

Enjoy! Have a zuri day!

Zuri Day

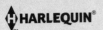

INTRIGUE

USA TODAY BESTSELLING AUTHOR
JULIE MILLER
RETURNS TO *THE PRECINCT* WITH A TALE OF A KILLER ON THE LOOSE AND A TORNADO ABOUT TO HIT KANSAS CITY

There is no way Deputy Commissioner George Madigan is going to let his beautiful assistant fall prey to a stalker. Because Elise Brown isn't just another employee. Her vulnerable blue eyes trigger all of George's protective instincts…and now her life is in jeopardy.

Working together almost 24/7 to bring the perp to justice—and sharing kisses passionate enough to ignite a Kansas City heat wave—George and Elise forge the kind of partnership that could keep her out of harm's way and potentially lead to happily-ever-after.

Until a deadly tornado strikes and Elise is taken hostage…

KCPD PROTECTOR
BY JULIE MILLER

Only from Harlequin® Intrigue®. Available August 2014 wherever books and ebooks are sold.

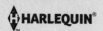

INTRIGUE

**IN LISA CHILDS'S *SHOTGUN WEDDINGS*
MINISERIES, A CONFIRMED BACHELOR
MUST WALK DOWN THE AISLE TO PROTECT
HIS NEWBORN SON**

Someone is trying to kill bodyguard Parker Payne. But what's
more shocking is the woman who shows up claiming he's
the father of her child. The baby boy is Parker's spitting
image, but how could he have forgotten a passionate
encounter with this woman with caramel eyes?

Sharon Wells has raised Parker's son since his birth. Now
with a homicidal maniac coming after her and her son, it's
Parker's unexpected proposal that may be the real danger.
Sharon knows Parker just wants to protect them. But with
passion flaring and a murderer intent on completing his
personal mission, any distraction could mean the difference
between life and death.

BRIDEGROOM BODYGUARD
BY LISA CHILDS

*Only from Harlequin® Intrigue®. Available August 2014
wherever books and ebooks are sold.*

ZURI DAY

THE NANNY GAME

Recycling programs
for this product may
not exist in your area.

ISBN-13: 978-1-335-58130-3

The Nanny Game

Copyright © 2022 by Zuri Day

For questions and comments about the quality of this book, please contact us at CustomerService@Harlequin.com.

Harlequin Enterprises ULC
22 Adelaide St. West, 40th Floor
Toronto, Ontario M5H 4E3, Canada
www.Harlequin.com

Printed in U.S.A.

Zuri Day is the award-winning, nationally bestselling author of a slew of novels translated into almost a dozen languages. When not writing, which is almost never, or traveling internationally, these days not so much, she can be found in the weeds, literally, engaged in her latest passion—gardening. Living in Southern California, this happens year-round. From there it's farm to table (okay, patio to table—it's an urban garden) via her creative culinary take on a variety of vegan dishes. She loves live performances (including her own), binges on popular YouTube shows and is diligently at work to make her Ragdoll cat, Namaste, the IG star he deserves to be. Say meow to him, stay in touch with her and check out her exhaustive stash of OMG reads at zuriday.com.

Books by Zuri Day

Harlequin Desire

The Eddington Heirs

Inconvenient Attraction
The Nanny Game

Sin City Secrets

Sin City Vows
Ready for the Rancher
Sin City Seduction
The Last Little Secret

Visit her Author Profile page at Harlequin.com, or zuriday.com, for more titles.

You can also find Zuri Day on Facebook, along with other Harlequin Desire authors, at Facebook.com/harlequindesireauthors!

Through mutual attraction we come to believe
It's better to give than it is to receive
To embrace a moment too magic to name
When life is the focus. And love's not a game.

One

"Au revoir, Desmond. À bientôt."

"Oui, mon amour, Penelope," Desmond replied, with an extra notch of bass in his voice. "Yes, I'll see all of you very soon."

"Oui, oui." Her soft, low seductive laugh oozed from the receiver and settled into his groin, signaling an end to business executive Desmond Eddington's long day. The week had been grueling, yet productive. For the past three months he'd been so caught up in overseeing the company's latest offering, Eddington Enterprise's own unique brand of cryptocurrency, E-Squared, that his love life had taken a serious hit. Been virtually nonexistent. An unexpected weekend tryst with one of his favorite lovers from around the globe was the perfect way to celebrate. It was such an exciting prospect Desmond decided to not even go home and pack an overnight bag. After placing several reports and his tablet in a lightweight briefcase, and adding Penelope's name to the guest list for his grandmother's seventy-fifth birthday bash happening tomorrow, he left his office.

"Pack up, Janice. It's time to go home."

His secretary, an older woman with a pair of glasses perched on the tip of her nose, kept her attention on the computer screen as she typed. "It's only four o'clock."

"Start your weekend early. It's been a long week."

Her fingers stilled as she lowered her head slightly to look over the rim of her half-moon glasses. "Are you feeling okay?"

Desmond enjoyed a hearty laugh. Workaholic that he was, her question was a relevant one. He gave her shoulder a squeeze and continued toward the elevators down the hall from where she sat.

"I feel great! Never better!" He reached the hallway and turned around. "So much so that I don't have to see you Monday until noon."

"Whoa, what?"

Penelope had a healthy sexual appetite and for him it had been a while. Considering that her flight wasn't scheduled until Monday evening, Desmond might need a little extra time off as well.

"You heard me."

"Are you sure you're okay? Come back here and let me check that forehead for a fever."

He stepped into the elevator with a laugh. "Enjoy your weekend!"

Desmond walked through the office building's main lobby and entered the underground garage looking like a cover model for a fashion magazine. The valet had timed the executive's departure to perfection, pulling up before Desmond's custom-made Carthay dress shoes left the building's outer-carpeted landing and reached the concrete edge.

The young man, dressed simply in the employee black-

and-gold uniform despite the increasingly frigid January-in-Illinois air, gave a slight bow as he exited the car and held the door. "Good evening, sir."

"Where's your coat?" Desmond asked, handing over the Italian leather trench he hadn't bothered to don to be placed in the back seat.

"Doesn't work with the uniform," the kid replied.

Desmond's unexpected yet welcomed date tonight was too hot for the cold to affect him. The nine-figure projected first quarter earnings boosted by the company's successful foray into cryptocurrency had the industry smoking. That the black Bugatti trimmed in platinum silver was toasty warm didn't hurt, either. Professionally and personally, the man was on fire!

"In weather like this, you need to be wearing an overcoat," Desmond said while sliding a hand into his pants pocket, pulling out a money clip and handing two crisp one hundred dollar bills to the surprised employee. "Buy one before Monday. Wool. Black."

He eased down onto the heated leather seat and briskly rubbed his hands together.

"Yes, sir. Thank you, Mr. Eddington! Have a great weekend!"

"That's exactly the kind I have planned." Desmond put his metallic monster into gear and rolled out of the parking lot. A light snow dusted the well-maintained streets of Point du Sable, an ultraexclusive neighborhood located at the edge of Lake Michigan and a stone's throw from Chicago's city limit. Desmond barely noticed. His mind was on Penelope, the Parisian vixen who'd enchanted him a year earlier during an impromptu Fashion Week trip to La Ville Lumière, France's premier city of lights. She was a seductive model and a fluent conversationalist, stellar company during the designer's private after-party where they'd danced away the night and part of the morning, both on the mansion's heated terrace and later in the boudoir. Busy schedules and an ocean between them made dating a challenge but they'd stayed connected through social media, phone calls and the occasional meetup in one of several playgrounds for the wealthy that dotted the world. The last time Desmond had seen her was in South Africa for a prince's wedding. Tonight she was in Chicago, making her acting debut in a project she promised to share more on over dinner. She promised to share herself for dessert. Desmond reached a traffic light. Instead of turning left toward Eddington Estate, he turned right toward Point du Sable's Main Street and the highway heading into Chicago. He'd just reached the light across from that said highway's on-ramp when his phone rang. It was Chauncey, the house manager, keeper of secrets, the Eddington family's all-around protector.

"What's up, Chauncey?"

"Good evening, sir. I tried to reach you at the office. Are you headed home?"

"As a matter of fact, no, I'm not."

A short pause and then, "You need to come home, sir. Right away."

Desmond frowned. "Why?"

"It's a rather delicate matter, Desmond, one best discussed in person."

"About what?"

"A delivery addressed to you, sir."

Is that all? The light turned green. Desmond crossed the street, entered the on-ramp and pressed on the gas to merge ahead of the line of cars behind him.

"What can be so delicate about that? Look, I'm headed to Chicago and will probably be gone for the weekend.

Have one of the runners place the box at my side door, or if the weather might affect it, put it inside the garage."

"Sir, this package requires your most urgent and immediate care."

Desmond released a short quiet sigh. Chauncey's dedication and attention to detail are what helped the family's estate run with such ease. But sometimes the concern and overly protective nature of the staffer who'd known the family since Desmond's dad, Derrick, was a young boy could be stifling.

"Chauncey, I'm sure you can handle it."

"I cannot, sir. This delivery is totally and completely out of my league."

"How do you know that? Did you open the package?"

"It is a box and yes, I opened it."

That wasn't unusual, either. Whenever a letter, package or box looked suspicious, security checked the contents before the goods were released.

"So, what are the contents and why do I need to see them right now?" Desmond steered around a car doing about seventy and resumed the eighty-five miles an hour his sports car seemed to prefer.

"Chauncey? Did you hear me? What's in the box?"

Chauncey cleared his throat. "A baby, sir."

Had this been a movie, this moment would have called for a loud screech sound effect. As it were, Desmond eased off the gas and gently pumped the brake. Obviously, driving fast affected his hearing. And while the luxury sports car steered so smoothly it practically drove itself, Desmond's fingers gripped the wheel.

"A what?"

"A female infant that Bernice figures is around a month old."

Bernice was Chauncey's much-beloved wife and head

of housekeeping. The two had joined the family as a package deal more than twenty-five years ago.

"Addressed to me?"

"And a sealed envelope inside bearing your name as well."

"From whom?"

"There is only a company name on the return address— Acting Up, LLC."

Shelly. Desmond's heart almost seized in his chest.

"The package was dropped off about thirty minutes ago by a young uniformed driver in a white nondescript van. However, it wasn't checked until approximately ten minutes ago when the child who'd likely been asleep when delivered woke up and began making a fuss."

As Chauncey spoke, Desmond crossed three lanes of traffic to take the next exit and raced back to Point du Sable. He was less than ten minutes from the Eddington compound when a thought hit him smack upside the head. The only one that made sense in the plethora of those that had jumbled his brain since getting Chauncey's phone call. This baby delivery was a joke. An elaborate, effective one no doubt spawned from the mind of Jake, his younger brother. Wasn't it just last week while visiting with Jake's best friend Cayden and Cayden's expecting wife, Avery, that Jake had teased Desmond about being next in line for the husband/father role? Desmond's shoulders relaxed as a smirk graced his face. He was tempted to turn around yet again and head back to Chicago. But being so close to home, he decided to personally relieve Chauncey and the staff of their anxiety and pack a few toiletries and other personal items for the fun-filled weekend ahead.

Of course, Jake was behind this madness. The irascible asshole had been a prank-playing pain in his side almost since he could walk. It was either him or his sidekick best friend Cayden, the family's brother from another mother. Desmond tapped the phone icon on his steering wheel and placed a call to the office.

"Jake Eddington."

"Dammit, Jake. Good try but not funny."

"I don't know what you're talking about."

Desmond's phone pinged. Penelope. Good thing he'd waited to call her to cancel the weekend. Their rendezvous could continue as planned.

"Hold on, Jake." He tapped the icon. "Un moment, chéri." Then back to Jake. "Where'd you get the baby?"

"Baby? What baby?"

Crap! Desmond checked the screen. The call hadn't switched over. Penelope was still on the line. He smacked his forehead and inwardly cursed. His hot date had almost received a cold dash of baby news that neither needed.

"Je suis ton bébé. Ne suis-je pas?"

In imagining those soft, cushy pillow lips prettily pouting, Desmond shook his head as the thought of a wild ride on the Penelope side seemed intent on fading faster than invisible ink. "Of course, you're my baby," he responded, continuing their conversation in flawless French.

"Are you on your way?"

"Soon. There's a slight emergency I need to handle."

"But you are coming, no?"

"Absolutely. I plan to come more than once."

"You're such a bad boy." A smile replaced the pout in her voice. "Our dinner reservation is for seven o'clock."

"I'll be there."

Desmond ended the call, double-checked the screen to make sure Jake and not Penelope was still on the line. He even managed to produce a grin at his brother's crazy antics.

"Look, bro, the scheme was elaborate. Finding a child, having it sent to my address. Wild and crazy even for you and I appreciate the effort. Still, my wager from last week stands. You'll likely become a father before I do and when that time does come, my child will definitely not be delivered via a mailing service. You need to have that kid picked up and returned to its mother."

A second passed.

Then five more.

"I don't know what you're talking about."

Desmond's smile faded. "Come on, dude. We're getting too old for these kinds of games."

"I'm not playing with you, Desmond. I know nothing about any type of delivery, and I damn sure haven't been anywhere near a baby, unless you count the one Avery is carrying right now."

"Man, you're good. I almost believe you."

"Swear to God, Des. I've been at the office since seven this morning and will likely still be here for a while."

"Where's Cayden?"

"He and Avery left for an impromptu trip to California this morning. You can't blame this one on Jake and Bake."

That meant Shelly, his longtime friend with benefits, was the culprit? It wasn't like her to joke around. Not like this. What would be the point? They hadn't spoken that much lately or seen each other since she'd suddenly packed up and shipped off to Hollywood determined, she'd said, to become an A-list movie star. That was about…nine or ten months ago. Memories of their last few times together began to play like a movie reel inside his head. As Desmond neared the guardhouse by the family compound's imposing wrought iron gates, a feeling of dread pooled in the pit of his stomach. If what seemed impossible just seconds ago became possible now, Desmond Eddington was about to lose more than a bet.

Two

Ivy juggled a bag of salad fixings as she worked to retrieve the ringing phone from a purse swinging precariously off her shoulder. She snatched it out just before reaching the door that led from the garage to the kitchen.

"Hello?"

"Ivy Marie Campbell. Whew! I'm so glad you answered."

"Hey, Lynn. I just got home. Hold on." Ivy opened the door. She held the phone against her ear with her shoulder while walking through the laundry room, navigating around the spoils of her mom's latest shopping spree left in the hallway and setting her groceries on the kitchen counter.

Her mother, Helen, yelled over the sound of the TV show she was watching. "About time you got back. What did they have to do to make that burger, butcher the cow?"

Oh, shoot. "One more minute, Lynn. Don't hang up!"

Ivy hit the mute button and entered the living room. "Sorry, Mom. After getting through that long line at the DMV and stopping by the store, I forgot all about your sandwich. I'm about to make a salad with roasted chicken, though. How does that sound?"

"Like something I don't want to eat. I swear you'd forget your head if it wasn't screwed on."

"Even attached I've still come close a time or two." Ivy gave a smile she didn't feel. Evidently her mother found no humor in the comment, either, which when it came to Helen's mood seemed to be standard operating procedure these days.

"I can go back out for your burger."

"Never mind. Just make mine a chicken sandwich, with mayo and a slice of cheese. And bring me a soda and that bag of chips."

"Sure, Mom." Ivy unmuted her phone. "Lynn, can I call you right back?"

"This can't wait. I have a job lined up and they need you right now."

"Seriously? Okay, hold on."

Being in her mother's home for the past three months had brought back all the reasons why Ivy had been happy to leave it in the first place. Helen was still the bitter, demanding, ungrateful woman who'd raised her. Living life on her own terms in college and beyond, away from the negativity, had given Ivy a new lease on life. Meeting Gerald had felt like yet another bright beginning. Then tragedy struck. Her world got upended. Yet even with the devastating accident that separated her from the man she believed to be the love of her life and created the shield around her heart, and while her mom's home had been a hiding place of sorts from those wishing her harm, she couldn't wait to move out again. The sooner she began working, the faster that could happen.

"Give me a sec, Mom. I'll make your sandwich right after finishing this call."

Ivy hurried into the guest room that had become her refuge and gently closed the door behind her.

"Okay, Lynn, thanks for waiting." She placed the call on speaker. "I might have a job?"

"Not a job, a career, one that could potentially secure your future earnings for the next eighteen years."

"But I just sent over my résumé and interviewed with you last week!"

"I know and trust me, that was a good thing. How quickly can you get to my office?"

Ivy checked her watch. It was after seven o'clock on a Friday night. "I can come by first thing Monday morning. What time do you open?"

"We open at eight, but I need you here now. This position must be filled immediately, with employment beginning as soon as possible. How soon can I expect you?"

"I'm on my way."

Ninety minutes after that phone call and a hastily made sandwich, and thirty minutes from leaving Lynn's office, Ivy took the exit for Point du Sable, a tony, ultraexclusive incorporated town just north of Chicago that boasted some of the state's wealthiest residents. She was still reeling from the quick chain of events that had her about to be interviewed by one such family—the Eddingtons. Though not famous in quite the celebrity sense, and whether or not one was wealthy enough to require their financial services, most Illinoisans at least knew who they were. Ivy certainly did. Like scores of other women, she'd drooled over the pictures of the stately and handsome Derrick Eddington and even more so his two sons, Jake and Desmond. And like most of those same women, she'd assumed that mental fantasies of them being together was as close to one of them as she'd likely get. Yet now here she was, heading to Desmond's home to meet the family and interview about becoming nanny to a child. His child, she assumed, although even after signing the nondisclosure agreement, Lynn had been less than forthcoming with the information Ivy felt she had a right to know.

"They'll explain everything," is how she'd answered Ivy's questions on Desmond's marital status and whether or not the charge she would be caring for was his child.

"And remember," Lynn had added when they reached her outer office door. "All information received for the purpose of handling your employment obligations will be held in the strictest of confidences."

"Of course."

Ivy hadn't understood Lynn's attitude, but kept quiet about it. It wasn't like the news wouldn't eventually get out. Who in the world could hide a whole baby?

She reached a guardhouse next to an intimidating pair of wrought iron gates, a grand entrance to a cluster of homes—mansions, according to Lynn—collectively called the Eddington Estate. A uniformed gentleman with the bearing of a military general slid open his window. She lowered hers, letting in a blast of icy air.

"Good evening. May I help you?"

"Yes, I'm Ivy Campbell, here to see Desmond Eddington."

"Your ID, please?"

"Sure." Ivy retrieved her driver's license from its pouch in her wallet and handed it over.

"One moment, please."

Ivy watched the man pick up the phone and make a call while copying her ID. While it wasn't her first time entering a secure community and knew such actions were normal, they still felt like a violation of her privacy, such as that was in today's information-driven world.

He returned to the window and held out her license.

She lowered hers and retrieved it.

"The directions to the home you'll be visiting have been texted to your phone through an internal navigation system. Just click on the link and follow the instructions. Have a good evening."

The text message dinged as she pulled out her phone. The wrought iron gates opened with such majestic flourish it deserved a musical accompaniment. Her fingers tightened around the wheel as she left regular civilization and entered an earthbound paradise. Everything awed her. Each home she saw was grander than the last. When she reached Desmond's address, a contemporary multileveled masterpiece located in a cul-de-sac at the top of a hill, it took her breath away. Ivy had thought Lynn's requirement of wearing a suit to the interview over-the-top. She was being interviewed for the position of nanny, not a corporate exec in the Eddington firm. Now, however, the navy wool suit she'd paired with a white cashmere turtleneck gave her confidence and felt appropriate for the opulent surroundings.

Following the navigational instructions, she continued around to the home's parking area. Across the way was what Ivy assumed to be a detached garage that she guessed could hold at least six cars. She pulled into the parking space closest to the main house's side entrance and reminded herself to breathe as she tried to adopt a professional decorum. Hard to do when one felt like Cinderella about to meet a prince—one handling a baby instead of giving a ball.

Not a prince. Not a date. Your potential employer. One likely married with a newborn. Stay focused!

Those thoughts stilled the butterflies, along with reminding herself that she was on break from dating, maybe permanently. A romantic entanglement was far from her mind. After a quick check of her makeup in the rearview mirror, Ivy secured a woolen scarf around her neck, exited the car and hurried up a walkway lined with snow-dusted evergreens. Just as she reached a gilded door made of ebony wood, it swung open.

"Ms. Campbell?"

"Yes."

"Come in, darlin', and close that door before we freeze to death."

Ivy complied, barely able to take in her stunning surroundings before being prompted down a short, wide checkered floor hallway.

"I'm Bernice," the woman said as she hurried them along.

"Desmond's mom?"

"Ha! I wouldn't have any problem owning that title except a woman named Mona would have a serious problem with that!"

They reached the end of the hall and turned into a beautifully appointed living space. Ivy entered and stopped short as five sets of eyes turned in her direction. Before she could recover and offer a greeting, a man for which the cliché tall, dark and handsome was almost an insult looked up from his phone and stood to greet her. A near imperceptible once-over preceded a brief smile that shot like an arrow straight to her heart and caused a heat that chased away the winter chill while eliciting its own set of goose bumps. She didn't realize she was staring.

"Hello. I'm Desmond Eddington."

"Ivy Campbell."

"Thanks for coming on such short notice."

Ivy shook his outstretched hand and answered with you're welcome or no problem or something similar. Or so she hoped. Swear to goodness when she looked into his twinkling deep brown eyes surrounded by long curly lashes, she forgot that English was her first language. The practical thinker prone to indifference gave way to a woman who within seconds had fallen in lust.

Right away, Ivy knew two things for sure. One, the on-line photos of Desmond, while magnificent, had not done him justice. Two, if the way her body physically reacted to his presence was any indication, she was in big, big trouble.

"Let me introduce you to the family."

Bernice stepped up. "Ivy, let me take your coat."

She slipped off her bulky down jacket, very aware of Desmond's penetrating gaze. She handed off the coat and walked with Desmond over to a seating area with a couch and matching loveseat, and two expensive-looking wing-backed chairs, the only seats open. One was where Desmond had been sitting. The other, she assumed, was for her.

They stopped at the loveseat "Ivy, this is my mom, Mona, my dad, Derrick, and my sister, Maeve."

Ivy noted the similarities between father and son. Mona could have been Maeve's sister.

"Nice meeting all of you."

Desmond extended an arm toward the sofa. "My brother, Jake."

"A pleasure meeting you, Jake."

Jake stood, offering a wide grin and a firm handshake. "I don't know how pleasurable any of this is, but we're definitely glad to see you."

This earned a tsk from Mona along with a quietly delivered single command. "Behave."

"This is Chauncey, half of the duo that heads up the support team holding this estate together."

"And I'm the other half," Bernice added, before taking a seat beside him.

"Have a seat, Ivy."

Ivy noted that Desmond seemed much more serious than his brother. She sat in one of the accent chairs. Desmond sat in the other one.

"Where's Reign?" Jake looked at his watch and toward the front door.

"London," Mona answered, followed by, "Another of your sister's wild hairs. Don't ask."

Again, all eyes returned to Ivy, stirring up the butterflies. She'd expected a one-on-one interview with Desmond and considering the circumstances, perhaps his wife or mother. Not half of his family and definitely not the help. Is this how the elite did things? Ivy wasn't sure but...okay.

"Do we have her NDA?" Desmond asked.

Mona nodded. "She signed it, son."

"I'd like to see it, please."

Bernice stood. "I'll go get it."

"I'm sure Lynn emphasized the sensitive nature of the matter we'll be discussing."

Ivy nodded at Desmond, hoping to add assurance with a slight smile. "She didn't provide many details but yes, she made sure I knew that whatever we talked about would remain confidential."

"Before we get further into the interview, do you have any questions regarding the nondisclosure agreement?"

Ivy shook her head. "It was very straightforward."

"And you understand the repercussions of that not happening? How you'll be sued for breach of contract and prosecuted to the full extent of the law?"

The blatant threat took Ivy aback, not to mention the arrogance she perceived. Even with the incredible salary, she wasn't sure this was the type of employer she wanted or, if hired for the position, a job she should take.

Her expression remained neutral, even stoic, as she conducted a visual assessment of her would-be boss. He was arrogant and flashy, she thought, adding those undesirable traits to the arsenal she was building against other unwanted feelings. The watch he wore had a face outlined in diamonds, the price of which Ivy imagined could pay off her student loans or buy a house. Her pragmatism deemed it ludicrous to wear a residence on one's arm when there were people across the country sleeping in tents. According to Lynn, the Eddingtons had made their money by being savvy, astute, brilliant businessmen. Ivy guessed that fact afforded Desmond the right to do what he wanted with what he earned.

Most women in his circle probably salivated in his presence, but Ivy wasn't impressed. Much.

"Brother, we've barely begun the interview. Please don't scare her away."

"Thanks, Maeve," Mona responded to her daughter before turning her attention to Ivy. "I'm sure Desmond trusts Lynn's agency and this process. It's been a very trying and eventful day."

"One that leads me to be extremely cautious," Desmond said. He looked at Jake. "The background check?"

"No criminal record, not a skeleton to be found."

He stared at Ivy. "Anything not on record that we should know about?"

"Like what?"

"Like anything."

"No."

"You sure about that?"

Ivy had had enough. She stood abruptly. "Perhaps it would be best if you found someone else."

"Give her a break, Desmond," Derrick chided. "She answered your question. Let's move on."

"Please," Mona said to Ivy. "Have a seat."

Ivy sat on the edge of the couch. The tension in the room could be cut with a knife. She thought of her reason for being there and decided to not take Desmond's rude behavior personally.

"I imagine this overcaution has to do with your baby?"

"Who said anything about the kid being mine?"

Damn if he wasn't even sexier when frowning than when he smiled. Intimidating, too, but Ivy wasn't one to be bullied.

"I thought that's what Lynn told me. Was she wrong, or did I make an incorrect assumption?"

"Not exactly," Mona offered.

Jake shrugged his shoulders. "We don't know."

Amid the uncomfortable silence that ensued, Bernice returned with a folder that she handed to Desmond.

He took it and after scanning the contents, settled against the chairback. "Earlier today, a box addressed to me was delivered at the guardhouse. Inside was a baby—"

"The child arrived by courier?" Ivy was astonished.

"With a note saying the child was mine. I don't believe it."

Any nervousness Ivy experienced was replaced by outrage. She stared at Desmond, wide-eyed. "Excuse my outburst, but did you say that an actual baby was dropped off via a delivery service?"

"Given how incredulous the news seems to you, imagine how I felt."

"This child was dropped off randomly, by a stranger?"

"Yes. And the note was from an on-and-off girlfriend I haven't seen in months."

Like around nine months, maybe? Instead of voicing this thought aloud, Ivy simply responded, "Oh."

Desmond fixed Ivy with a look that made her want to squirm. She'd never been this close to someone so incredibly good-looking, physically perfect as far as she could tell. Had never experienced such a visceral reaction to another human being. But there was something about Desmond that was magnetic and mesmerizing, drawing Ivy to him like a moth to a flame.

A fire you'd better put out and quickly, girlfriend, so you can focus on getting this job.

Maeve cleared her throat. "It is very important that our family maintains the stellar reputation for which it is now known. There are a number of reasons this incident must remain private, one of which is that my brother is an esteemed member of society, a mentor to young men, and a business and civic leader. It would be the highest of scandals and a stain on our name if what happened today becomes public. If proven true and the child does belong to Desmond, the PR narrative created will require a deft hand."

"How do you know Lynn?" Desmond asked.

"We met at a social event a few years ago, then reconnected through social media."

A slight rising of the eyebrow suggested to Ivy that this was news. It was probably a rare moment when the meticulous businessman left a string dangling but now seemed to be one of those times.

Despite her obvious, growing discomfort, Desmond continued to grill her. After several uncomfortable minutes, Mona intervened.

"We need someone who is excellent with children," she said. "Your résumé and Lynn's recommendation makes us secure about your ability to handle the job. But more than that or anything else, we need someone who can be trusted completely."

"Is that you, Ivy Campbell?" Desmond turned to look at her fully.

She swallowed and nodded. "That's me."

"Good." He smiled and Ivy swore the room brightened.

"Now, tell me why a woman just shy of a doctorate degree wants to babysit a newborn."

A sharp pang hit her heart as Gerald's face swam before her, accompanied by other equally painful memories of why she'd left her life in Atlanta behind and returned to the Midwest.

"I've always loved children; babysat for several neighbors from the age of thirteen. By the time I graduated high school, I was certain that working with young minds, in one way or another, would be my life's work."

Ivy's nerves settled and her confidence increased as she settled into the topic of childcare, familiar ground.

"Good babysitters are major helpers to humanity," she finished, believing her brief presentation had gone over well. "We help pliable, gullible helpless babies become intelligent, well-rounded, contributing human beings."

When finished, Jake, not his brooding brother, was the first to respond. "Sounds like you definitely know your stuff. Yours or not, bro, clearly the kid will be in good hands."

"I'll admit your education is impressive. Which makes you leaving school so close to earning a Ph.D., and taking a job as a nanny, even more puzzling. I can't help but believe there is more to the story."

Another wave of sadness washed over Ivy. Her reasons were personal, and she wanted to tell him so. Discussing her all-too-recent heartbreak wasn't something she'd planned. But the question was a legitimate one and she needed the job. She glanced from Desmond to Mona, whose look of calm compassion gave Ivy the strength to tell the truth, albeit as little as possible.

"I, um, endured a tragedy recently," she said softly, forcing the words past the lump in her throat. "I was engaged. My fiancé…died."

Appropriate condolences were heard as through a fog. With Desmond's prodding she shared a bit more information, but soon the interview got back on track. Back to where Ivy needed to keep her attention so that she wouldn't break down. As long as she could keep the conversation geared toward being a nanny and raising a baby, and not on her deceased fiancé, his grieving parents or her potential charge's devilishly irresistible father, the better off both Ivy and her already hammered heart would be.

Three

Two days after being blindsided with a box of baby, a day after practically sleepwalking through his grandmother's celebration and less than an hour after Penelope cursing him out in multiple languages for standing her up and ruining her weekend, Desmond received the DNA news he'd dreaded, the information that left no paternal doubt. Penelope had thought her plans had been upended? She had no idea.

Desmond hadn't wanted to believe the report. Hadn't uttered the child's name until he knew for sure, and still hadn't held her. Staring at a copy of the irrefutable proof, however, reality sank in.

He was the father.

He had a child, a daughter, named Desiree.

Despite the ugliness of the situation, and the child's mother's irresponsible and selfish actions, he thought Desiree a beautiful name. Inspired by his name according to Shelly, whose real name was Michelle.

Shelly. He'd known her for years, had met her at the Boys and Girls Club where his dad used to volunteer when Desmond was a kid. Desmond would often ride over with his father. Shelly would always be there.

"Why are you always hanging out here?" he'd asked her.

She'd shrugged and answered, "No place else to go."

That's how their friendship started. It grew over a love for sports, hip-hop and video games. Shelly was smart, especially in math, which boosted her star power in Desmond's eyes. While being a popular student and an all-star athlete, Desmond broke the dumb-jock stereotype by also graduating with a 4.0, a GPA he maintained throughout college. After high school, the two lost touch. They reconnected at a party two years later. The friendship turned flirty and eventually physical, though the two never actually dated. Instead, a friends-with-benefits situation developed, with the two seeing each other a few times a year. Desmond wore a condom every time they had sex. Every. Single. Time. As he had with every woman he'd dated since his sexual exploits began. It's a message his father had drilled into his head, and Jake's, too. No babies out of wedlock. Derrick never judged others who chose to behave differently but it wasn't the Eddington way.

So how was it that he'd become a father? How had one of his tadpoles managed to slip past the latex to become a part of the two percent—pregnancies that occurred even when a condom was used?

He'd done as his father instructed and the worst had still happened. Derrick had shown support over the weekend, but Desmond could feel his father's disappointment. Especially now. Derrick was being considered as a nominee for the presidency of one of the most powerful, influential and elite organizations in the world. The success of E-Squared Cryptocurrency had the financial world's spotlight shin-

ing squarely on both the family and Point du Sable. That
he'd failed his father and possibly jeopardized the spotless
Eddington name hurt more than Shelly's betrayal.

Desmond reached for one of three papers on his desk.
The lavender single sheet outlined in flowers had a jag-
ged edge, suggesting that it had been torn from a journal
or notebook. The loopy writing was the same as what had
been written on the box that had forever changed his life
when it was delivered.

Des: Please don't hate me for getting pregnant and
not telling you. I thought I could be a single mother
and when it became clear that I couldn't, it was
too late to terminate the pregnancy. This is your
daughter, Desiree Michelle. Please take care of her.
Shelly…

Desmond's team was currently about the business of en-
suring that this whole matter would be properly handled.
So far Michelle "Shelly" Washington was MIA, but Desmond wasn't worried. Much. He'd hired one of the best and
most discreet private investigation agencies in the world.
He had no doubt that if Shelly was anywhere on the planet,
they'd find her. His only concern was that they reached her
before she told anyone about his involvement. He didn't
think she'd do anything crazy, like try and blackmail him
for instance, but he couldn't speak for her friends.

He set down the note, bypassed the DNA results and
picked up Ivy's résumé. Since their meeting two days
ago, she'd stayed on his mind, probably more than a mere
nanny should. He remembered his body's reaction when he
first saw her, how he'd been struck by a feeling not easily
named. She was an attractive woman in an understated,
unassuming way. Nothing like the models and celebrities

he dated, many, he imagined, with stylists and makeup artists. Ivy's radiance came from an inner quality, one that calmed his spirit even as it intrigued him. When their eyes met, it appeared she'd felt something, too. Her reaction had been subtle—a brief hesitation in her step, the quick flutter of lashes—but he'd seen it. His sisters would have attributed it to what they'd dubbed the *Easy E*—an effortless, sexy, captivating charm that they swore the Eddington men had in spades. Mostly, he would have agreed with them. To say that women tended to act mesmerized around them was simply the truth. But he wouldn't be so quick to say that applied to the new nanny. She seemed the no-nonsense, practical sort.

But could she be trusted? She'd signed the disclosure, said she understood it, but he still wasn't convinced she could practice the type of discretion and maintain the type of privacy the family and especially this sensitive matter required. Then there was the matter of her personal life and the tragedy she'd only recently endured. Was she truly in the mental framework to make this long-term commitment, one that could bind her to the family for at least the next five years? Desmond continued to stare out the window as he remembered the rest of the interview.

"How do you know Lynn?" he asked.

"We met at a social event a few years ago, then reconnected through social media."

This was news. He'd assumed that Lynn, his buddy's wife, had grown up with Ivy, or that they'd gone to school together, but hadn't been able to ask Isaac directly. He couldn't. Outside of Lynn and Ivy who'd signed NDAs and the child's mother, no one knew he was a father. Until their PR story was absolutely flawless, Desmond wanted to keep it that way.

He asked if she understood the NDA. Ivy said she did.

"I hope so. Because any leaked information about my household, this estate or the baby you're hired to care for will result in immediate termination."

His words caused Ivy to sway backward. Desmond didn't blame her. Instead of assuaging her uneasiness, he'd added to it. He'd spoken more strongly than intended but meant every word. Then entertaining another possibility, his shoulders tensed. Women had used all kinds of tactics to get close to him. Could this be one of them?

"Lynn just met you?" he queried, the smile gone from his voice.

"We met a few years ago."

"Where?"

"A First Friday event."

"Excuse me for saying so but you don't seem to be the First Friday type." He ignored his mom's covert warning glance and continued to press. "Where was it?"

Ivy scrunched her brows, shooting a slightly perplexed glance to his mother. Mona shifted as she eyed her son, but said nothing.

"Well?"

"As I said, it was a while ago and you're right, I don't attend them often. I believe it was at Lake Chalet, a boutique hotel on—"

"I know where it is. Where are you from?"

"I was born in Gary, Indiana, and grew up in Chicago."

"Does your family still live there? Do you have siblings? A boyfriend or disgruntled ex we might have to worry about if you take this position?"

Taking in Ivy's obviously increasing discomfort, Mona interrupted with a gentle hand on her forearm. "Dear, what I believe my son wants is more of a personal background, so that we can know you better. Professionally, you seem more than qualified for the position. Why don't you tell us a bit about who you are, and why someone with your educational background would want to become a nanny?"

Desmond grunted. "The money, of course."

He saw, almost felt, Ivy bristle at his words. He didn't care. In for a penny, in for a pound.

"Or some other...ulterior motive." He crossed his arms and fixed her with an accusatory stare, watched her square her shoulders and secretly admired the unwavering expression she returned.

"I believe at some level most people seeking employment have a financial incentive."

Desmond grunted. "I'd say. At the salary we're offering to fix bottles and change diapers, I know a couple corporate execs who'd vie for the job."

"Desmond..." Mona warned.

"Besides wanting to earn a living, my only motivation," Ivy continued, emphasizing the last word, "is my love for children. I babysat all through middle and high school. Those experiences helped me decide on child education as a career. My dream was...is...to someday open a school for girls, with an emphasis on those from disadvantaged backgrounds."

"Then why aren't you pursuing a teaching career?"

"I am. If accepted for this position, Mr. Eddington, your child will be my first student." Ivy sat back and crossed her arms.

Mona and Maeve smiled. Jake chuckled. Desmond stewed. So far he couldn't detect anything devious in her answers. But the interview wasn't over.

He picked up her résumé. "It says here that you were attending Georgia State, and working toward your doctorate?"

"Yes. I am very close to completing that degree."

Ivy proudly rattled off her educational accomplishments. For Desmond, taking a break while being so close to completing such a lofty goal was an immediate red flag. He felt there was more to the story and pushed for full disclosure. In hindsight, he almost wished he hadn't. Finding out her fiancé had been killed changed the atmosphere for everyone.

"His loss was sudden, unexpected and left me without the clarity and discipline needed to complete my dissertation…or anything else."

"I'm so sorry for your loss," Mona said sincerely.

Desmond shifted in his chair, the first sign of discomfort from him all evening. His eyes softened, even warmed, as he looked at her. "My deepest condolences, Ivy. That had to be tough."

"I can't imagine," Maeve added. "You have my sympathies."

Jake shook his head, his eyes full of compassion as he mumbled, "Damn."

Desmond watched Ivy's jaw tighten, to rein in her emotions, he imagined, as she rapidly blinked her eyes. The feelings of suspicion were replaced by those of compassion, and a desire to pull her close to him and wipe any tears that might form from her eyes. These were not the usual thoughts entertained while interviewing an employee. Added to the unexplainable desire of wanting to get to know her, now this enigma of a woman was bringing out his sentimental side.

Subconsciously, his heart made the decision before his head had a chance to rebut it. She didn't need to know that, though. With a face devoid of emotion, his attention returned to the conversation as Ivy shared more of her personal background and what led her to choosing childcare as a lifelong career. He listened, but where she grew up and why she chose her college major no longer really mattered.

Interrupting the segue into her choice for higher learning with a dismissive wave, he said, "You're hired."

Her eyes brightened. "I am?"

"You are," he said, before looking at his watch and standing. "Since my mom and Bernice have been handling the baby, I'll leave them to handle the rest of the interview. Chauncey, you're excused as well."

The gentlemen stood. Chauncey bowed his farewell and departed. Desmond offered a serious look along with his hand. "Welcome to the Estate."

With a kiss to his mom's forehead raised in surprise, Desmond had left the room. His strides had been long and purposeful, those of a relaxed, confident man. But truth be told, he was nervous. He felt like running. Away from possible failure. Away from home. Away from a baby. And away from the inexplicable, unexplainable way that Ivy made him feel. On one hand, her proficiency left him with the hopeful belief that he, the family and the company would survive this dilemma with their earnings still climbing and their social status and reputation intact. On the other, she was a stranger. An outsider. One about to become a part of his household, holder of secrets, bound only by her character and the indelible ink on an NDA. She'd come across as one possessing those solid traits Midwesterners were known for—being honest, hardworking, levelheaded. But the world could be cruel, the corporate world, cutthroat. He had to know he could trust her completely, that she understood that the stakes were extremely high. Sometimes wolves came in sheep's clothing, especially those itching to knock the Eddingtons off their throne. Desmond had made a huge mistake trusting Shelly. He couldn't afford to make another.

Four

Ivy secured a strip of tape over the box's seam, then looked around the now-almost-bare spare guest room. She frowned, something that happened often since her meeting with Desmond. Almost two days had passed since her interview with the Eddingtons and while she'd immediately fallen in love with Desiree, her cherub charge, the brusque way Desmond had questioned her still rankled. That and how many times a day he crossed her mind in ways that had nothing to do with employment.

At first, she'd been able to convince herself that it was because she'd gotten the position to be Desiree's nanny, an important step to the process of leaving her mom's home and rebuilding her life. Then she told herself it was because he was a jerk. That as handsome as he was on the outside, the way he'd grilled her during the interview provided a glimpse of ugliness within. Finally, she'd remembered Gerald, her ex-fiancé, and the drama with his family, and how her having any type of success or happiness at all was totally unfair. Those reasons were somewhat true, but not the crux of the matter. No, the central point of her discomfort was how inner muscles tightened and feminine flower lips moistened when she thought of Desmond's smile and those sexy eyes, and the slender athletic body that Lynn had suggested could play any sport. Everything about him was unexpected—his presence, looks more startling in person than from afar and the insane attraction she felt for him from the moment their eyes met and fingers touched. A ridiculous reaction, even if his deep voice sounded like a bridge over troubled waters and came with a smile that could cure Covid. Desmond Eddington was the type of man that a woman like her could only dream about. Fortunately, Ivy's focus was secured in reality. She was seeking a potential employer, not a romantic interest. Even if looking for the latter, which she wasn't, given a broken heart still needing to heal and a skittishness toward close-knit families, she'd hardly go for someone like the smooth, suave, successful panty moisturizer from a clan the Kardashians would need to keep up with, instead of the other way around.

Mona had texted to let her know that Bernice was caring for the baby and would be on hand to help settle her in. Ivy would do well to keep her mind squarely on Desiree and whoever was coming by to help her get settled, and not on the little angel's dad.

Still, she would have had to have been born without senses to meet Desmond in person and remain unaffected. From the curly brown hair to his designer-clad feet, Ivy was hit with raw maleness, smoldering sensuality, almost overwhelmed with the alpha-ness of it all. Broad shoulders. Strong back. Long legs. Tight ass. Smooth dark skin that reminded her of her favorite chunky chocolate gelato and made her want to lick him like an ice-cream cone. She had just two words for that up-close-and-personal intro. *Gor. Geous.* Damn! She'd been ready to jump the man, wrestled with at least a dozen improper thoughts before a word had been spoken between them. That was totally out of character. She wasn't like those silly women given to flights of fantasy. She was practical, conservative, strictly type A. Yet, it had taken effort for the real Ivy to jump back in her body and replace the imposter who'd felt like a hormonal, overreacting teenager seeing her first crush. Desmond Eddington was out of her league. Above her station and pay grade. Given his undoubted extravagance and her practical nature, Ivy felt that suited her just fine. She'd pack up her life and relocate to the Eddington Estate in Point du Sable to be his daughter's full-time live-in nanny. Whatever this attraction that was as crazy as it was unexpected, she had less than eight hours to get it in check.

After loading her car, taking a shower and experiencing a fitful night's sleep, Ivy awoke to a text.

Good morning, Ivy. Bernice is under the weather and I have a prior daylong commitment that missed making my calendar. Bernice's granddaughter, Sabrina, and one of our house staff will be waiting with the baby and will assist you in moving into your new home. I have included our butler, Chauncey's number for all other needs and will touch base with you tonight. Mona

"Good," Ivy mumbled, ignoring a pang of disappointment as she walked to the closet. Perhaps it was better to be greeted by Sabrina on this auspicious day than by the perfectly put together Mona or her handsome hunk of a son. She'd be lying to say a part of her hadn't wanted to see him again, to find out if he'd found a manner or two in the days since they'd met. She bypassed the stylish khakis she'd pressed last night and planned to pair with a funky cropped sweater and reached for a less fashionable but more comfortable burgundy sweat suit. Instead of the cute ankle boots with a clunky wooden heel she thought might impress Mr. GQ, she slid socked feet into the cozy pair of UGG boots she preferred. After pulling her hair into a ponytail and her toiletries into a large shoulder bag, Ivy took a last look around the room and headed out the door. A dusting of snow had fallen with a chance for more. Ivy wanted to leave early and get ahead of the storm. She also wanted to avoid waking her mother. They'd enjoyed a civil dinner and said their goodbyes last night. Helen had seemed less than impressed with Ivy *paying all of that tuition to end up babysitting*, but acted happy to once again have the house to herself. Ivy wasn't sure she believed that and had encouraged her mother to seek out friends that existed outside of her fifty-inch screen TV, but craving her own independence, Ivy understood her mother's position and chose to leave on a positive note.

Thinking about Mona's text on the drive from Chicago to Point du Sable, Ivy became less disappointed and more grateful that Bernice's granddaughter, Sabrina, was meeting her and she wouldn't have to deal with Desmond first thing. Or Mona, for that matter. As kind as she'd been throughout the interview process, Ivy was über-aware that the dynasty's matriarch was used to having and wielding unquestioned authority. It wouldn't be good to cross her. Ivy would use the time alone to get acquainted with Desiree and to acclimate and settle into her new surroundings. Her employer's suave charm (when he wasn't being a jerk) and good looks (she couldn't imagine him having a bad hair day) awakened parts of her she hadn't known existed. This way her focus would be exclusively on getting to know little baby Desiree and settling into her new home.

She approached the gate with the thought sinking in that within this idyllic paradise was the place she'd call home for the foreseeable future. A pleasant conversation with the guard while he set up her facial recognition ID calmed her nervousness. She followed the GPS around to the circular drive behind Desmond's home. Grabbing her bulky coat and pulling it around her, she dashed up to the private entrance of the downstairs suite, home— she smiled at the thought—and rang the bell. In the cold weather, it felt like several minutes passed rather than the few seconds that had actually gone by. She rang the bell again and was about to ring it a third time when the door was jerked open.

"You're early."

"Oh!" Not the person she expected. Ivy's eyes widened and averted at the same time, but not before glimpsing a scowling Desmond with glistening wet curls and a tightly pulled robe over the manly chest that had haunted her dreams, which suggested he'd just gotten out of the shower. She thought about her casual attire and wished she'd been wearing her sexy boots.

"Well?" His scowl deepened. "Are you trying to warm up all of the outdoors?"

"My apologies. It's snowing and…I left early to avoid traffic…"

"Don't worry about it." He stepped back.

She entered. "Where's Bernice?"

"With the kid. We need to talk."

"I'd prefer to wait until you're dressed," she responded, inflecting hints of the same sharp tone he'd used the other day—not only to match his gloomy mood but to cover the fact that she was as attracted to him today as she was on

Friday. If they were going to work together, he needed an attitude adjustment and she needed to rein in her mind, body and soul.

Even as she thought this, she looked down and saw that her nipples had pebbled to attention and were protruding like headlights against her top. She pulled up her coat to cover them and looked up to meet Desmond's blazing gaze.

He raised a perfectly arched brow, his twinkling eyes conveying the humor he obviously felt but that she missed completely. What he did to her was no laughing matter. Ivy wasn't exactly a prude but seeing even a hint of her boss's hard chest and smooth skin did funny things to her insides.

"Or if you'd like, I can wait outside." She began to ease into her coat.

"That won't be necessary. I won't be long." He retrieved a cell phone from the robe's pocket. "I'll get someone to come down and help with your things. You did come prepared to stay awhile?"

His sexy wisp of a smile sent Ivy's heart skittering across her chest, even as it somewhat relaxed her. A little. "Yes."

"I'll be right back." Desmond finished sending a text. He took a couple steps toward the stairs, then turned. "Sorry for snapping at you earlier."

He blessed her with another one of those almost smiles and disappeared up the stairs. *You're pitiful*, she thought, as blatant desire rippled through her core. She sighed like a smitten schoolgirl in spite of herself.

Five

Ivy forced herself to not watch his retreat but could imagine those long legs and that hard-looking butt mounting the stairs. To divert her attention, she took a turn around the elegant, well-appointed room, like something you'd see in a five-star hotel. The soft ivory, tan and light blue color combination was soothing. So beautiful were her surroundings that she almost pinched herself to know that what was happening was real. She went to the window where the snow that dusted her car on the way over now turned to big wet flakes settling on pine trees in varying hues of brilliant green. She thought of her ex and the life they'd planned. The accident that took his life and changed hers forever. His parents, and their ugly accusations. Memories stilled the time as her mood shifted. It didn't seem right for him to be gone and this paradise to be her new life.

"One of the staffers is on his way to unload your car."
Desmond's voice startled her, but it was nothing com-

pared to what his appearance did when she turned around. In his navy suit, baby blue-colored shirt and striped tie—tailored to perfection—he looked like the boss that he was, and like the breakfast she should have eaten but in her haste to beat the possible snowstorm had failed to consume. It took everything within her not to gasp and stare agog. Instead, she turned and sat on one of two plush chairs covered with the softest leather she'd ever touched before her legs failed her.

Desmond sat opposite her. "Mom said I was a bit hard on you yesterday. Do you agree?"

Absolutely! Ivy thought this, but carefully crafted her answer and hoped it would lead to more information. "It became clear that the situation concerning your daughter is a serious one, and quite sensitive as well."

"Extremely. In the wrong hands or released prematurely, the news of my having a daughter could negatively impact—everything—the company's bottom line."

"Is that what matters most to you?" The question came out before she could stop it.

His eyes narrowed. "What matters is that my privacy, and that of my family, is strictly maintained. For other reasons I don't wish to get into right now, your assessment of this matter's sensitivity is a correct one. I want to underscore the importance of confidentiality regarding everything related to your employment, this home and the Estate."

He stood. "Everything that happens regarding this family is to be held in the strictest of confidences. Do you understand?"

"Yes." She was too angry to trust anything more coming out of her mouth.

"Good." The doorbell rang. "That's probably one of Chauncey's assistants to help with your things. Sabrina is on her way to show you around. If you need anything, let her know."

Before she could respond, Desmond was gone and the doorbell was being rung again. She answered it. Two staffers introduced themselves as the ones he'd ordered to unpack her car. While the men emptied her car, a process that took all of five minutes, a heavily bundled young woman pushed a stroller through the opened door.

"Whew! It's cold out there!"

She yanked off a knitted cap to reveal a mass of natural curls, pulled off a pair of matching mittens and eased out of her parka, chatting all the while.

"Sorry to barge in, even though the door was open. I see the guys are helping unpack. They're the best. Did you see Desmond? Mona will be back in a couple of hours."

Ivy stood taken aback by whirlwind Sabrina, amazed she'd followed the conversation even though the young woman hadn't taken a breath.

Leaning over the stroller, Sabrina pulled back a heavy blanket and cooed. "Hey there! Ready to come out from under all those covers?"

Sabrina jerked upright. "Oh, my goodness, the weather has frozen my brain." She walked over to Ivy. "I'm Sabrina. Chauncey and Bernice are my grandparents."

"Ivy Campbell."

"It's so good to meet you. Even though I'd actually rather continue babysitting Desi than go back to college."

"Why don't you?"

"My dad would have a cow…literally."

"Angus or Wagyu?"

"Whichever is cheaper."

Ivy laughed out loud. Sabrina was like a breath of fresh air. It was easy to see why Mona liked her.

"How long have you known Desmond?"

"All my life," Sabrina replied with a shrug.

"Does he seem comfortable with Desiree?"

Sabrina hunched her shoulders again. "I've never seen him with her."

Ivy wanted to ask more questions about Desmond and the elite world of the Eddingtons, but she felt dangerously close to replacing legitimate information relative to her employment with pure gossip about the family of her smart, handsome boss. She steered the conversation back on the familiar territory of childcare. After giving a quick tour of the downstairs living space, which included a small kitchenette, Sabrina left. Silence reverberated around the walls. Ivy felt isolated and out of place. But not for long. Taking advantage of Desiree's nap time, Ivy kept herself busy to keep unwanted thoughts at bay. Wasn't hard to do. For all of her stellar head-of-the-class education, Ivy had little hands-on experience with children, especially infants. Her most recent interaction was with one of Gerald's cousins who she'd stayed with from the day his nephew had been born until the naming ceremony eight days later. Ivy, headed toward a doctorate in child psychology and development, was viewed by Gerald's cousin as an expert in childcare and had asked Ivy to assist her during this precious time. Ivy took the role seriously, making sure that the couple bonded with their newborn and creating a bible of sorts to take them through the child's first critical year. After unpacking and putting away her belongings, with her clothes going into a walk-in closet the size of her own mother's guest room, it was that bible she pulled up on her tablet to help formulate a plan and organize the space in a way that worked best for her.

Once finished with what felt like a doable plan for the next three months, Ivy pulled out last night's leftovers from the meal with her mother and had lunch. Mona called, apologized for being MIA on her first day and extended an invite for the following morning. It seemed Ivy had blinked and it was nightfall. On top of that, she was hungry again. Her meals were covered in the contract, but Sabrina had left without giving a full tour of the home, especially the upstairs—Desmond's domain—and Ivy didn't feel comfortable wandering around on her own. So far Desiree had been an ideal baby, only crying when hungry or wet. Ivy went to check on her. Clean, dry and full of milk, the baby enjoyed another round of napping. While pondering whether or not to bundle her up for a food run or have something delivered, her phone rang.

She pushed the speaker button. "Hey, Lynn."

"Hi, Ivy. How's it going?"

"So far so good. Except I'm hungry and contemplating whether to opt for delivery or bundle up the baby and go out for food and fresh air."

"Definitely have something delivered. It snowed all day and the temps are dropping again."

"I live in a fortress. How does that work?"

"Most deliveries are dropped off at the guard shack. One of the workers can bring it to you."

Ivy remembered Mona's earlier text. "You're right. I'll call Chauncey. He'll tell me what to do."

"Did Mona visit you today?"

"She texted her unavailability earlier today but invited me to breakfast tomorrow."

"Good. What about Desmond?"

Ivy sighed, walked over to three separately framed yet connected pieces of beautiful artwork and studied their intricate design. "What about him?"

"Have the two of you had a chance to talk today?"

"Desmond doesn't talk. He grills and commands."

Lynn chuckled. "It may come off that way, but don't take it personally. He's been a boss since birth."

"All he seems concerned with is his reputation and keeping Desiree a secret."

"This is all very sudden and a huge adjustment. I'm sure he's still trying to take it all in."

"What happened that he ended up being a single father with a baby?"

"Why don't you ask him, Ivy?"

"Yes, why don't you?"

Ivy gasped and whirled around. "Desmond! I…didn't hear you come down."

"Because you were too busy breaking your agreement by gossiping about me."

"Desmond, it's Lynn Martin, with the agency."

Stating the obvious sounded stupid, not at all like someone months away from a doctorate degree.

If either heard Lynn's loud declaration through the speakers, they ignored her. Ivy's attention was on Desmond, slowly coming toward her. To say he looked unhappy would be the grossest understatement of the year.

He stopped a few feet from her and spoke with an icy calm. "Since you feel qualified to question my parenting, why not ask me directly about whatever it is you want to know?"

Six

Desmond hadn't meant to eavesdrop. The day had been a decidedly more positive experience than the weekend he'd endured, though yesterday had felt more normal than any moment since the call from Chauncey about a package left for him. It had started off beautifully with several games of tennis before showering and dressing to the nines to attend his grandmother's birthday brunch at the esteemed Point du Sable Country Club. Afterward, he'd joined several buddies at a private men's club in Chicago, one that came with a hefty six-figure annual membership fee that effectively weeded out those of a lesser echelon and class. It felt good to feel normal, almost like his old self. By the end of the evening, he'd been able to largely forget that a daughter had been left on his doorstep and a stranger now shared his home full-time. That the fleeting thoughts of fatherhood that did make their way past his mental guard were less about Desiree and more about the nanny watching her was a conundrum he wasn't ready to tackle. Ivy was nothing like the women he dated, not his type at all. Why or how she'd wormed her way into his consciousness was something he didn't understand. He did, however, want to ensure their professional relationship was a pleasant one, which is why, while putting in a full day at work, he'd called the chef and planned to be home for dinner so that he and Ivy could spend time getting more comfortable around each other. It was obvious his world was a foreign one to Ivy and the world of fatherhood was equally strange to him, so his plans seemed fitting. Now, he felt the trust the NDA encouraged and his mother supported was misplaced. Barely forty-eight hours had passed since she'd moved into his home and already talking about him behind his back had begun.

Even so, when he should have been focused solely on throwing out the traitor, he was struck with the fearlessness in those big brown eyes, her luscious lips quivering ever so slightly before she bit down on her lower one, the way her chin tilted up in defiance.

He came to within a few feet of her, delicately close to her personal space, and crossed his arms.

"Lynn, I'll call you back." Ivy ended the call. "That was Lynn Martin from the agency."

"So I gathered."

"I wasn't gossiping about you. I was answering a question. She asked me—"

"I heard what she asked you. Even more importantly, I heard your answer, about being commanded and grilled, and how I'm not a father. How dare you speak on matters you know nothing about."

"She asked what I thought. As the person responsible for me having this job, and the information regarding it, I felt it right to share my opinion."

"You were disclosing that which you agreed not to disclose."

Stated in a way that brooked no argument. Ivy remained silent. He narrowed his eyes in response to her silence.

"You're right," she said, after a pause too long for his taste. "It was a prematurely formed opinion, one that even though asked, I did not have to share."

"First day on the job and already I could sue you."

"For what?"

"Breach of contract! One pursuing a doctorate degree is obviously smart. What part of the word *confidential* don't you understand?"

"I didn't think offering my opinion was breaking a confidence, especially since it was in response to a question asked by the agency that brokered this hire."

"Something tells me I ought to fire you right now."

"I'm truly sorry. It was wrong of me to speak out like that."

That she capitulated so quickly was a bit disappointing. To someone like Desmond, a strong backbone was as attractive as a woman's ample breasts or curvy butt.

"However," she continued after taking a breath, "if instead of speaking honestly you'd rather have someone who only says what you want to hear, then—" she swallowed "—maybe it's best that I leave. If a yes-man, or woman, is what you want…I'm not it."

Silence bellowed. Tension crackled in the air. Several seconds passed before unexpected sounds shifted the focus. One, Ivy's stomach growled, long and loudly. Two, Desiree began to whimper.

Ivy's eyes widened in embarrassment. "Excuse me!" She pressed a hand against her midsection. "I need to tend to your daughter."

"Fine. Do that. Dinner is served in an hour."

A slight tightening of her jaw and straightening of her spine told Desmond she wasn't quite the wilting flower he'd imagined just seconds before.

"Thank you, but I was planning to have something delivered."

"Change those plans." He turned to go. "One hour," he threw over his shoulder at her retreating back. "Don't be late."

Upstairs, Desmond paced his massive master suite. His anger at Ivy was convenient but misguided. It was wrong of her to be discussing him with anyone, and he'd make sure she knew that. But it was actually the situation of newfound fatherhood that had him on edge. That and dealing with a bundle of emotions foreign to this alpha male, ones that even now he covered with misplaced anger at Ivy, like uncertainty, vulnerability and fear. When it came to his professional and personal reputations the stakes couldn't have been higher. His being the face of the company's cryptocurrency, E-Squared. His father being considered for president of arguably one of the most exclusive and prestigious organizations in the world. Desmond had never failed at anything. Yet, here he'd been thrust into the most important job of his life, with no learning curve or ramp-up period provided. The truth of it was that Desmond felt completely inadequate when it came to handling a baby. He'd remedied that by not handling her at all.

That's why he'd hired Ivy.

Remembering the chef would be arriving soon, Desmond entered his dressing room. He changed from one of the exquisitely tailored suits he was known for and donned a more casual black turtleneck and jeans. While doing so he thought of the overqualified nanny now sharing his home. Was the death of a loved one, even a fiancé, really enough to cause someone a semester away from a doctorate degree to change their life course so drastically? Or was there another reason? It wouldn't be the first time a woman had used an ulterior motive to try to get close to him. He'd seen the flicker of attraction in Ivy's demeanor before she donned a mask of indifference. Desmond wasn't so arrogant as to think it wasn't possible for a woman to not be interested in pursuing a relationship. It's just that in the thirty-one years he'd been on the planet, he hadn't yet met that woman.

Desmond rubbed a hand over his five-o'clock shadow as he headed downstairs, his thoughts still on Ivy. Even with his suspicions of her motives, her credentials were impressive. He hoped she was there solely for Desiree, and that theirs could be a solid partnership when it came to raising the child. Ivy could very well be the key to not only getting through this challenge, but to Desmond learning how to be a dad. With that in mind, he determined to change his attitude and rein in his suspicions. No sooner had he done that, though, when the sound of tinkling laughter drifting down the hall had him frowning again.

He entered the dining room and saw the chef talking with Ivy. Her manner was relaxed, her smile broad as she listened to him. It was a casual, almost playful demeanor she'd not used around Desmond, a fact that shouldn't have mattered, but it didn't feel good. Upon her seeing him, the laughter stopped. The chef stopped talking. Desmond felt his recently tamped down suspicions rise again, especially when he saw a foreign device on the table.

"What's that?"

"Baby monitor," Ivy replied. "Desiree just had her bottle but in case she wakes up, I want to be able to hear her."

Desmond turned off the paranoia. It was the only way any type of trust could be established and since this woman would be living in his home, trust was what he'd need.

"Good evening, Desmond," John said, pulling out the chair at the head of the table.

"Evening, John. I see you've met Ivy."

John nodded.

"What were you doing, sharing family secrets?"

"Of course not, sir."

"Then don't stop talking on my account."

"I was just mentioning how little Desiree will soon have a cousin playmate."

"Yeah, Cayden is still a kid at heart himself. I can't imagine him being a dad."

Cayden Barker, Jake's best friend, brother from another mother and notorious playboy, had surprised everyone the year before when he met a former employee at the Point Country Club and eloped six months later. The bun currently in Avery's oven had stunned the newlyweds as much as the announcement about their nuptials had shocked everyone else. As much as learning about Desiree had surprised him, Desmond reckoned.

"I have a bottle of cabernet breathing," John said. "Should I pour you both a glass?"

Desmond looked at Ivy.

"None for me, thanks."

"You don't drink?"

"Technically, I'm on the clock."

"Your boss won't mind if you have a glass."

"In that case, yes, I'll have one. Thanks, John."

John left the room. Desmond returned his attention to Ivy. His offer of wine wasn't simply based on him being a good host, but on hoping a bit of alcohol might loosen her up, bring back the carefree spirit he'd spied upon entering the room. The woman before him now was quiet, guarded, nothing like Penelope the Parisian or the type of woman he usually dated. Ivy was an attractive woman, no doubt about that. But hers was a quiet, unassuming beauty. Still waters that he found himself wanting to dive into and find out how deep they ran. Enticing, though she hardly wore any makeup at all. Wholesome is how he could describe her. A thought that made Desmond smile since it was a word that usually didn't accompany situations with Desmond and the opposite sex. But there was something intriguing about her. Something challenging about the way she'd recovered earlier when he'd confronted her, adopting a professional veneer as cool as a dipper of water from an Alaskan stream. During the interview, she'd mostly interacted with Mona (and since his mother had led most of the interview, he guessed that was only fair), causing him to second-guess how he'd interpreted her initial reaction, one of at least a hidden attraction as was the case with most other women. Not that any of this mattered. Along with the matter of the abject impropriety of sleeping with the help, their burgeoning cryptocurrency business and his father's consideration, not to mention the unexpected delivery on his doorstep, his casual dating door had been effectively shut and locked.

Ivy took a sip of lemon water from the crystal goblet nearest her, then squared her shoulders and met his unflinching gaze.

"I want to apologize for the conversation you overheard earlier. Even though it was not meant to be mean-spirited, I understand how it must have sounded from your point of view."

"No one wants to be talked about behind their back. Especially someone who has signed a legally binding document to the contrary."

"Again, that wasn't my intent, but I understand your reaction. I was hired through Lynn's agency and provided an honest answer to a question I thought benign."

"I hear you." Desmond believed her. Decided to let her off the hook. A person on the defensive might find it harder to open up.

John returned with the wine, a basket of warm bread and two dressed salads. He filled their glasses and offered fresh cracked black pepper before retreating from the room as quietly as he'd entered.

Desmond lifted his wine glass. "Bon appétit."

"Thank you." Ivy took a small sip.

An awkward silence followed.

"Please, help yourself. I know you're hungry. Those warm rolls will melt in your mouth."

"That was embarrassing," Ivy said, obviously remembering her stomach's hungry growl. She reached for a piece of herbed yeasty goodness and slathered on butter. Desmond followed suit.

Ivy moaned.

Desmond's thought upon hearing her audible appreciation had nothing to do with food. He stabbed and ate a hearty bite of salad just to distract himself. For the next few minutes, the sounds of clinking silverware were the only ones heard.

After finishing their salads, Desmond reached for his wine. "Okay, let's talk about what you said to Lynn, all of this grilling and commanding of which I've been falsely accused."

Ivy reached for her wine as well, took a couple contemplative sips. "Just as I didn't intend to come off as disloyal to you, you may not have meant to sound like a drill sergeant."

Desmond rubbed his chin. "Continue."

"I felt as though I were on trial and given the ninety-day probationary period written into my contract, I guess

I am. All the more reason why I felt Lynn's questions deserved answers."

"What you call grilling, I call direct questioning."

"What you see as backstabbing, I call honest conversation."

Desmond's face remained passive but his insides smiled. Clearly, there was something about Ivy Campbell that he liked. Intuition was a large part of his business acumen. He decided to go with it.

"Believe it or not, I can understand that as well. What do you say we call a truce and start this relationship over? As you can probably imagine, this development has placed me under a great deal of pressure. With the recent passing of your ex, perhaps you're feeling the same."

Her relief was palpable. "I'd like that."

Desmond extended his hand. "Hello, Ivy Campbell. I'm Desmond Eddington and it is my pleasure to meet you."

After a brief hesitation, she grasped his hand. Hers felt small and warm and soft. The electricity was there—invisible yet unmistakable. He resisted the urge to rub his thumb across her hand and instead released it with a reassuring squeeze.

"What would you like to know about me, Ivy Campbell?"

She responded without hesitation. "How did you become a single father?"

"I'm still trying to figure that out," was his honest answer. "Desiree's mother and I practically grew up together."

"She lives here, in Point du Sable?"

"I'm not sure where she lives now."

Ivy gave a slow nod.

"She grew up in Chicago. Her uncle owns a high-end

automotive dealership and serviced many of the town's residents, including my dad."

"That's how you two met?"

"That's how my dad met her uncle. She and I met at the Boys and Girls Club, where my dad was a mentor for many, many years and still sits on the Board."

He paused as John returned to remove their used plates and serve up the main course—strips of thinly sliced Wagyu beef atop a bed of wild rice and roasted brussels sprouts.

"Oh, my gosh, what is this?" Ivy asked after the first bite, the topic of baby's mother temporarily forgotten.

"Breedlove Beef, some of the best meat that could ever cross your palate. We get it shipped directly from the ranch where the cows are raised, a family-owned outfit in Nevada with international acclaim."

"It's so tender, and flavorful. I'm usually not a big fan of red meat, but I could eat this every day of the week."

"Glad to hear it. Before scheduling dinner, I didn't think to ask your food preferences."

"I'm not a fussy eater," Ivy replied after another mouthful. "I'll try almost anything once."

Again, Desmond's mind drifted from the topic at hand as he imagined pleasurable first-time uses for her delectable lips.

"I'm sorry, we were speaking about Desiree's mother and why the child is with you and not her. This was obviously not a mutually agreed upon arrangement. Did something happen that prevents her from taking care of her daughter?"

"Your questions are legitimate but not ones I'm fully prepared to answer. Let's just say…it's complicated."

"Fair enough."

"That being said, I've fully assumed responsibility for

the child's welfare with the goal of helping her to grow into a happy, well-rounded, successful adult."

"Is the mother in Desiree's life at all?"

"Not at the moment."

"I see."

Ivy's attention returned to her meal, a welcomed respite for Desmond from Ivy's questioning. He now sympathized for how she felt earlier, and the feeling that she was on trial. The plain truth of it was that Desmond knew very little about what was happening with Desiree's mother and had as many or more questions than Ivy. This conversation underscored that fact, along with the need to get answers.

"What about you?" he asked, refilling both of their wine glasses.

"What about me?"

"You mentioned losing your fiancé being the reason you left school. I realize this is a sensitive topic but…what happened? I'm assuming he was a young man."

"That's a very difficult subject for me to talk about."

"I understand. I only ask because of how hard it is for me to understand why someone just shy of their Ph.D. would agree to become a glorified babysitter."

Ivy visibly bristled.

"No offense intended," he quickly added.

Ivy finished her dinner, wiped her mouth and reached for the wine. "It was a car accident," she said at last, her eyes looking past him and into the memory. "Rain-soaked roads. Reduced visibility. A driver ran a red light. We were broadsided."

"How long had the two of you dated?"

"Almost five years. We met as undergrads, became serious while pursuing our master's. Gerald went on to law school, specialized in entertainment. My dream is…was…

to open a school for girls. The accident changed everything."

"I can't imagine losing someone so unexpectedly. Hopefully, being here can help with the healing process."

"Children are a blessing. I definitely believe Desiree will bring some of the sunshine back into my life."

As if on cue, a whimpering sound poured out of the monitor.

"Sounds like your blessing is waking up," Desmond said, with a nod toward the device.

"She's probably hungry. Would you like to come feed her?"

The mere thought was terrifying. But Desmond kept his cool. "That's what I'm paying you to do. I've got work," he added to calm the storm he saw brewing on her face.

He could fairly see the plethora of thoughts swirling around in her head, none he imagined too pleasant. She didn't voice any of them. It was almost disappointing.

"Thanks for dinner," she said.

She rushed off quickly, the monitor still on the table. Desmond finished his wine and headed up to his office, assured that with Ivy around his daughter, in a strange way, even his household was in good hands.

Seven

The rain fell heavily over the crowded streets of metropolitan Atlanta. Visibility was minimal, even with the wipers at top speed. Ivy weaved in and out of traffic, hoping to get to the store before it closed and back home before the storm warning turned into a flood warning.

"What's the rush?" Gerald asked her. "Where's the fire?"

Instead of answering his questions, she cursed at the driver of a car that had cut too close. Ivy gripped the wheel.

"Ivy, slow down."

"Okay."

She eased off the gas. They neared an intersection. The light turned yellow. Ivy sped up to beat the red light. Seemingly out of nowhere, a white truck barreled toward them. Ivy laid on the horn, then screamed upon impact. From what she remembered, Gerald never said a word.

Ivy woke up shaken and disoriented, clutching the quilt

around her. That was a dream? It had felt so real. The rain. Gerald's face. The scene playing out as detailed in the police report, as real as it was the week everything happened. Except she woke up. Gerald had not. She tried and failed to bring her emotions under control. Finally, she stopped trying. Allowed the haunting grief and guilt to spill out of her heart and onto her face, wiped away with one thousand thread-count Egyptian cotton sheets. She cried for everything she'd lost, for Gerald, for all that could never be. Memories spilled along with the tears, the words of accusation hurled at her from Gerald's parents echoing in her mind.

It's all your fault. It was storming. You shouldn't have had our son out there.

Their opinion was formed by grief and half-truths. The police report had made that clear. The other driver, not Ivy, had been at fault and ticketed. That didn't matter. Gerald was dead. The reality made her cry harder.

So much so that she didn't hear the light knocking on her bedroom door, didn't hear Desmond calling her name. Didn't hear the door open or his light steps cross the room. Wasn't aware that she was no longer alone until he raised the dimmer to a subdued lighting and neared her bed.

"Ivy."

She raised her head and gathered the sheet in one motion, pulling the latter against her scantily covered body. What was Desmond doing in her room? Could he possibly have heard her distress? She wanted to tell him to leave and go back to bed, that she was alright. She opened her mouth but instead of words, only anguished sobs escaped.

He crossed the room in long strong strides, gently sat on the edge of the bed nearest her and pulled her into his arms. In a move that was completely uncharacteristic, brought on no doubt by vulnerability the dream had produced, Ivy clung to his robe, her head buried against his chest as she worked yet again to stop the flow of tears.

"Shh, there now, it's going to be okay. Stop crying," he chided, his voice low and gentle, his hand cupping the side of her face as a thumb wiped away tears. "There's nothing to be afraid of here. You're safe, protected, I promise."

He positioned himself against the headboard, pulled her more securely into his arms and rocked her with a surprising tenderness. A move that made Ivy feel a plethora of emotions, all tumbling through her heart and head at once. She became aware of his even breathing, the slight rise and fall of a rock-hard chest. She took a deep breath and inhaled the subtle scent of a musky cologne. It awakened her femininity, her latent sexuality. It had been almost a year since Gerald had passed. There'd been no one else since that time. She'd thought that part of her may have died with him. But in this moment, there was no doubt that it was alive and well, her skin tingling, fingers itching with a desire, almost a need to run her hands across that chest and skim her fingers across his soft curls. She wanted to explore his lips with her own, see if they were as soft as they looked and if he was as skilled in kissing as he was in conversation. Then, as if reading her thoughts, she felt their softness against her temple. So light, it could have been imagined. Was it?

His hand ran back and forth across her back, then slowed. "Feeling better?" he asked, his voice a husky whisper.

She almost didn't want to admit it. Doing so might cause him to end the embrace, to pull them apart and deprive her of his magnetic warmth. But as the sad emotions receded, common sense returned. Reality drifted back in with stark clarity—that she was cuddled up next to her boss of less than forty-eight hours, wearing a wisp of a nightgown and not much else. She placed a hand on his robe, making sure not to touch his skin, and pushed herself upright. When he reached for a couple tissues in the case on the nightstand, she took the moment to scoot over and put even more distance between them.

"Here."

"Thank you."

He got up, went out into the suite's living area and returned with a glass of water. "Drink this."

Having added a quilt to the sheet covering her, she reached for the glass. Their fingers touched. Their eyes met. Hers dropped to his lips. In the moment, she wanted nothing more than to feel them pressed hard against her own. She took the glass and busied herself drinking the water, trying to get a whole pack of wayward hormones under control and praying he'd leave quickly.

"Sorry to wake you. I can't believe you heard me all the way up there."

He held up the monitor she'd left in the dining room, then set it on the table beside her. Only then did she realize she'd fled without it and that he was holding anything besides her body in his hands.

He leaned against the wall. "Want to talk about it?"

Was he kidding? The accident, not to mention its messy and ongoing aftermath, was the last thing she wanted to talk about, especially with her new employer. Where she was working needed to be as big a secret as the baby she watched. The tragedy that happened to Gerald was only part of the reason she'd left Atlanta. The other was Gerald's family, who'd maligned her name and pretty much ruined any chances she'd had of making a career there as she'd planned. The Russells were high society Georgians and well-connected, likely traveling in some of the same circles as the Eddington clan. Their finding out she worked for them was the very last thing they needed to know.

"Ivy?"

His silky voice brought her out of her reverie. "Not really."

"It might help." She remained quiet. "Was it a dream about your…about Gerald?"

"More like a nightmare. For the most part, I've forced myself not to think about that night and everything that happened afterward. All that talk during dinner stirred up unwanted memories, and obviously stayed on my subconscious mind."

"Sounds like it's my turn to apologize."

Ivy shook her head. "It's not your fault. My therapist in Atlanta warned against keeping everything bottled up inside."

"Are you still seeing someone?"

"She gave me a few recommendations for therapists in this area, but I haven't yet followed up."

Silence filled the space as Desmond walked to a high-backed corner chair and sat down, instead of out of the room like she wanted.

"Do you need more water?" he asked.

"No, thank you."

He crossed his arms and stretched his long legs in front of him as if he planned to stay awhile. She was fully covered but felt naked. He was at least six feet away from her, but her body throbbed as though they were mere inches apart.

"Tell me about him, your fiancé. What was he like?"

It was a sensitive, caring question that not even her best friends or mother had ever asked, at least not directly. In this moment, Ivy preferred the commanding, grilling Desmond to the sensitive man in her room right now, the one whose dark brown alluring eyes were filled with concern. Even through the residual turmoil, she was aware of how good he looked. A shiver ran through her that had nothing to do with the weather. The temperatures had dropped as Lynn had warned, but right now in her bedroom, Ivy felt nothing but heat.

"If you'd rather not…"

"No, I don't mind. Though, I am a bit shocked. Everyone has asked questions about his death, but not of his life."

Desmond noted her empty glass and got up to refill it. Ivy used the moment to pull her knees to her chest and wrap the covers more securely around her.

"We were a lot alike. I guess that's why we instantly connected and got along so good. He was quiet, introspective. But he wasn't a pushover. When Gerald wanted something, he went after it."

"And at one time, that was you."

His question brought warmth to her cheeks and to her heart as she remembered those early carefree days.

"Ours wasn't a fast earth-shattering romance. It was a love that blossomed out of friendship, shared goals and mutual respect. He could be a character once you got to know him, could do these spot-on impressions of comedians and actors he liked."

She remembered one he used to do of an Atlanta native who made it big and was surprised at the sound that escaped her lips. She hadn't laughed at a thought of Gerald in a very long time.

"What were his career plans?"

"He was on the fast track to becoming a great entertainment attorney. As you're probably aware, Atlanta is a mecca for that industry. Having been born and raised there, he knew a lot of influential people, ones with connections to the music and film industries, and the political arena as well."

"You must have been very proud of him."

"We were proud of each other."

Desmond nodded. "Sounds like you two had a bright future."

A bright future. That's how Gerald's parents had described his path, used those exact words and spent months blaming Ivy for snuffing it out. The warm fuzzy feeling that had cocooned her only seconds before was replaced by the cold accusations from an angry, grieving mom and dad whose actions and bad-mouthing had run her out of town. Would Desmond still respect her if he heard their version of the story? Would he still believe her to be the smart, responsible, capable employee he felt he'd hired? If he heard how they described her—irresponsible, irrational, reckless, deceitful—would he trust her behind the wheel with his child? It was a question, Ivy silently vowed, that would never have to be answered. If she had anything to do with it, any say-so at all, Desmond would never know further details from that fateful night.

"I think I'll try and go back to sleep now."

It was an abrupt, clear segue, but thankfully Desmond didn't object. He stood and walked over to where she sat in the bed.

"Are you sure you'll be okay?"

She nodded. "Thanks for coming to check on me." As a further act of dismissal, she fluffed the pillow behind her and sank into the downy mattress.

Desmond eyed her a beat longer before turning to leave. He reached the corner and said, "Do you want the lights off?"

"Not all the way. Maybe dim them to the lowest position?"

"You've got it. Sweet dreams, Ivy."

"Good night."

Her dreams were sweet alright. The nightmare of what happened to Gerald and his parents' aftermath was replaced by endless thoughts of being held in Desmond's arms. She felt guilty but couldn't help it. If she told anyone it had felt anything less than amazing, she'd be telling a big fat lie.

Ivy awakened disoriented. She was groggy and had a headache. Unusual. Then she remembered. Desmond. Last night. Dinner. The wine. The dream that became a nightmare. His body, hard, hers, left wanting. The genuine care in his voice when he asked about Gerald. A rush of emotions rose up within her, warring for attention. Remembering her breakfast meeting with Mona, she gratefully ignored them all, whipped out of bed and stumbled into the shower. After a couple of spins, Ivy exited the glass enclosure with its computerized system, dressed quickly, then dressed and fed Desiree. She'd assured Mona there was no problem in bundling up the baby and making the short drive over in her vehicle, but Mona insisted on sending a car instead. One look out the door once the driver arrived and Ivy was glad she had. The car was a Bentley, her first such experience. The SUV model she learned was a Bentayga drove as though they floated on clouds.

When Lynn had described the family's residences as mansions, she'd told the truth. Here, Ivy could shift from last night's nightmare into the dream of this place. The brick home showcased at the top of the land's highest hill was marvelous beyond imagination. A skillful combination of modern architecture combined with old-world charm, everything was stately and grand. There were wraparound balconies and large windows, one of beautifully stained glass that Ivy imagined let in tons of light. Even in winter, the landscaping was meticulous, majestic firs lining the roads and driveway, the topiary done on the fir shrubs a true work of art. The driver navigated the automotive wonder down the circular driveway to a motor court at the back of the house. The jaw-dropping beauty continued as she reached the solarium where Mona said they would meet. More like an architectural masterpiece, an exotic garden encased in walls of glass. The door opened before she reached it. Ivy encountered Chauncey's welcoming smile.

"Good morning, Ms. Campbell." He stepped back so she could enter.

"Good morning, Chauncey. And please, call me Ivy."

"As you wish. I see you've come bearing gifts."

"Gifts?"

Chauncey nodded toward the stroller.

"Ah, yes. A gift for sure."

Ivy followed the older straight-backed gentleman down a short hall and through a copious amount of potted trees and flowers, accompanied by the sounds of gurgling fountains (and birds!), to a cozy seating area near an enclosed double-sided fireplace. Mona sat at one of several small tables looking comfortably regal as Ivy approached. A tea service set on the stark white linen, along with several covered dishes.

Mona stood up when Ivy reached her and gave a brief hug. "Good morning, Ivy."

"Good morning, Mona."

"I'm delighted you agreed to join me."

"I was thankful for the invitation." Truly, she was thankful for the diversion—from Desmond and memories of Gerald and his family. More than Mona could ever know.

Mona leaned down and pulled the soft wool blanket away from Desiree's face. "And here's my little angel looking just like her father. She's sleeping so peacefully. I'll leave her be.

"Come, have a seat." Mona turned to Chauncey. "Thank you. We're fine for now."

Ivy sat in a wrought iron chair with a memory foam cushion and positioned the stroller beside her.

"Would you care for coffee, or tea?"

"Yes, tea. Thank you."

"I was hoping you'd choose tea. Do you like spices? Cinnamon, cloves, ginger?"

Ivy nodded.

"This is a special blend from Morocco that's to die for. Whatever it's dressed with—honey, lemon, sugar, cream—you can't go wrong."

"Sounds delicious."

"It's completely addicting. You've been warned. While I'm at it, I might as well put you on alert about Desmond, too, though you've caught a glimpse already. At times, he may come off uncaring or brusque, but inside that armor beats a very big heart."

"Good to know he has one." Ivy hadn't meant to voice the thought out loud. It escaped before she could catch it.

Mona laughed. "Good to know you have a high intellect and quick wit. With Desmond, you'll need both, encased in skin thick enough to withstand Lake Michigan. Naked. In the dead of winter. Understand?"

"Completely," Ivy answered, the argument with Desmond and the nightmare that followed fresh on her mind, softened by the memories from his visit to her bedroom.

"I might need to toughen up."

"This job, and the family that comes with it, will definitely help you do that."

The women continued chatting while dressing their teas. They went over the details of Ivy's job description

along with days off, sick and personal days, and vacation time. Ivy liked Mona. Without Desmond around, she relaxed completely and actually enjoyed chatting with the queen of Eddington Estate.

"Do you have any other questions for me?"

"Yes, and it's a bit of a sensitive one. Has Desmond spent much time with his daughter? He seems disconnected from her. I'm concerned at their lack of interaction."

"This situation was unexpected and new for all of us. It's a huge adjustment for the entire family. Desmond is used to being the expert, fully in control. In this fatherhood role, he's like a fish out of water. Unfamiliar territory for my son. He'd never admit it, but Desmond is terrified of that little girl, and between you and me, I think he's afraid of failing at something, which would be a first."

Ivy nodded in understanding. "Any suggestions on getting him more comfortable around her?"

"Getting him to hold her would be a start."

"He's never held his daughter?"

"No, but on its own that statement sounds worse than it is. He's only known about her for seventy-two hours. He's taken the paternity test and knows she's his daughter and being such, has taken her into his home and hired a very capable woman to help raise her. And, honey, believe me when I tell you, when it comes to men and responsibility, my son has done more than most."

Instead of Chauncey, it was Bernice who arrived pushing an ornately decorated cart with silver-domed trays from which the smells of goodness and mercy wafted past Ivy's nose. The conversation moved to more general topics, including life in Chicago, Ivy's doctoral pursuits and her dream of one day opening up a charter girl's school. Mona talked about her own degree in business, inspired by a dad who'd only recently retired after a certified public accountant career that lasted forty years, and how when she met and married Derrick, she gave up the corporate world without a second thought or backward glance. Ivy heard the pride in her voice when she spoke of Point du Sable in its early days and how in being some of the town's first residents, the Eddingtons had had a strong hand in shaping it into the crown jewel it now was in the arena of elite enclaves. All of this transpired as Ivy enjoyed some of the finest cuisine ever to pass her lips—a quiche so light, made with ingredients so flavorful and eggs so fresh she could almost imagine the chicken that laid them. Halfway through the meal, Desiree awakened, which pleased Mona immensely.

An hour and a half after arriving, Ivy left the Estate with less judgment about Desmond and the Eddingtons and more empathy for what it must be like for him to be navigating this unexpected interruption in his life. Back at home in her suite with Desiree plopped in a bouncer, Ivy thought about the child's mother and wondered what kind of woman could get pregnant with the child of a powerful man like Desmond, then leave her child in a box with a stranger at a guard shack. She was sure there was a story there but Ivy forced her thoughts away from speculation and made a conscious decision to focus solely on Desiree. That's whom she'd been hired to take care of, not the father. Aside from his need to bond with his daughter, how Desmond felt or what he did was none of her business, despite his bedside charm.

Eight

Desmond looked up from his seat near the fireplace in his father Derrick's study as Jake and Cayden entered the room. It was the first time all the Eddington men had been together since everything happened. He gave a slight nod to his brother, Jake, while greeting Cayden who'd reached him first.

"What's up, man?" Cayden asked, with a shoulder bump.

"Life," Desmond replied. "How was California?"

"Not as exciting as what's going on in the Point, from what I hear."

Desmond gave his brother a look. "Asshole."

Jake raised a brow. "What? He's family! You think he shouldn't know?"

"I think I should have been the one to tell him."

Desmond said this but didn't really believe it. Jake and Cayden had been best friends since they were ten years old. There were no secrets between them.

"I'm sorry, Des. I didn't think to keep it from him." Jake sounded contrite, which was rare.

"It's alright." Desmond let out a breath. "He was bound to find out sooner or later."

"Yeah, well, let's hope he's the only one."

"What's that supposed to mean?" Jake remained silent. "Bro, seriously, what have you heard?"

Jake gave a subtle nod toward their father, who'd ended the call he'd been on and now walked toward a minibar and poured two fingers of premium scotch before joining them in the seating area. He took a sip from the crystal snifter and stared into the fire. A feeling of foreboding spread from Derrick's throat to his gut.

"Who was that on the phone, one of the brothers?" Desmond asked, nodding toward Derrick's cell phone and referring to the elite fraternity known as the Society of Ma'at.

"Bob Masters," Derrick replied, sitting down on a customized brushed leather couch. "He called to lend his support to my presidential consideration. Wanted to give me the heads-up that this week he plans to announce his formal endorsement and offered to help wherever he was needed."

"Good man," Jake said.

"The best," Cayden added, smiling at the praise being heaped upon his mentor.

Relieved, Desmond walked over to the minibar and poured himself two fingers. He wasn't a heavy drinker but could easily see how others were driven to it.

After a fortifying sip, he asked, "Is the brotherhood all that was on his mind?"

Derrick sighed, threw back the rest of his scotch and grimaced at the slow burn the liquor induced.

"He wants to have lunch at the club tomorrow." He slid a glance in Desmond's direction.

Desmond's grip tightened on the snifter. Jake had just

alluded to the possibility that his secret was out. But how? He turned to his brother.

"Does someone outside of us know about Desiree?"

"Right now, it's all speculation. But it appears the delivery guy has been talking."

"Saying what exactly?"

"Nothing that can be proven. He told the guard about hearing a sound coming from the box. Joked about it sounding like a baby inside and it being a special delivery. The guard heard Desiree crying. That's why Chauncey was immediately called."

"Do we have the name of this guy?"

"We need to get it," Derrick interjected. "He needs to be shut up, and quickly."

"I'll speak to Sarge," Desmond said, referring to the guard on duty that day. "Everyone anywhere near that gate is on camera. He'll have a record of the company that was used, and the name of the driver."

"This couldn't have come at a worse time."

"I hear you, Dad. I'm so sorry."

"I'm not blaming you, son. Not singularly, anyway. You're as shocked as the rest of us. It's just a situation that has to be handled, that's all. We don't need this type of publicity right now."

Desmond couldn't agree more. When it came to his sudden fatherhood, he and his dad had yet to have a true heart-to-heart between just the two of them. Given Derrick's desire to lead the world's most powerful business society, the matter of Desmond's surprise baby had to be disconcerting. Then there was the Eddington legacy of being stellar fathers. They prided themselves on having children only with the women bearing their last names, a tradition that went back as far as it could in America, to documents that existed before the country was given that name. He was still baffled as to how Shelly had pulled off a pregnancy when he'd always used protection and she'd used birth control for years. That line in her brief note about thinking she could be a single mother nagged at him like a pesky mosquito. Did that mean she'd planned this pregnancy, that it wasn't an accident? Did she do the unthinkable as Jake had suggested and retrieve his condom after the deed was done? He couldn't imagine someone he considered a good friend doing something so scandalous. What would be the point? Shelly's family weren't in the Eddingtons' league when it came to prosperity but they weren't paupers, either. Plus, with Shelly's beauty, she could pull men with money from Chicago to Shanghai.

As if reading his mind, Derrick asked, "Have you had any luck locating her, the child's mother?"

Desmond shook his head. "A mutual friend is pretty sure she left the country. She'd mentioned plans along those lines the last time they talked."

"You've got Curtis handling it? His agency is one of the best in the world."

"Yes, and they've been working 24/7." Desmond frowned as he pondered the possibility of her not being located. "We need to get that NDA signed yesterday."

"And settle the matter of full custody. Michelle has proven unsuitable for motherhood. We can't trust her to raise Desiree properly and as an Eddington, the child must get nothing less than the best."

"I'm truly sorry, Dad," Desmond repeated, his voice barely above a whisper. "Not only for what happened but for the timing. Your campaign, the crypto surge focusing all eyes on our company..."

"I accept your apology, Des, but really, it's not necessary. Desiree is an Eddington and we will love her as such. Don't worry about the business. Money and morals are seldom playmates. As much profit as we're making for those investing, even with a little fallout, we'll be okay there. The same can't be said for the Society. If the secret gets out and her arrival turns into a scandal, my chances for becoming president are as good as dead. As for the child, I believe you when you say you used protection and know how scandalous women can be. Considering your eligibility, it's a wonder you made it to thirty-one before this happened. That said, we have to come up with a spin that places her unexpected arrival in a good light."

"A positive spin on sudden fatherhood with the mother MIA?" Cayden's expression showed the skepticism that others felt. "How do you plan to do that?"

The men looked at Desmond.

"That's the million-dollar question that when it comes to answering, I don't have fifty cents' worth of a clue."

"You've got that overqualified nanny helping you, Ivy. That should provide some comfort. You know she had breakfast with Mona today."

"No, didn't know that."

"Mona invited her up for a casual chitchat."

Jake gave a sarcastic chuckle. "Nothing Mama does is casual."

"Okay, she invited up Ivy for a reconnaissance mission. Does that sound more accurate?"

"Spot-on."

The room experienced its first true levity of the evening.

"At any rate, she's impressed with the young lady. Says Ivy is smart, focused and without ulterior motives, like snagging you for a walk down the aisle. When it comes to sniffing out those kinds of opportunists, your mother's a bloodhound. If anything other than that child was her priority, my wife would have picked it up."

Jake eased off the desk where he'd rested his hip. "I've gotta agree with Dad, bro. In all your years of friendship with Shelly, Mom never trusted that girl."

"Please, don't remind me." Desmond's phone dinged. His brows knit when he checked the face.

"Speak of the devil."

"No, it's Ivy. She's asking when I think I'll be home."

"Uh-oh." Cayden's eyes twinkled. "That sounds like a wifey question. Are you sure Mama Mona's gold-digger radar is working correctly?"

"Positive. Ivy isn't wired like that."

"And you know this already how?"

Desmond felt himself getting annoyed and defensive, which surprised him. "I just do."

Derrick looked at his watch. "Damn, had no idea it had gotten this late. I'm surprised Mona's not calling to question my whereabouts." He stood, stretched and looked at Desmond. "You probably should run home and check out what's happening. Knowing Ivy, whatever it is concerns Desi."

Despite the turmoil surrounding her presence, and the evening's revelations, the nickname his parents had given his daughter warmed a spot in his heart. Surprisingly, the thought of Ivy waiting at home for him warmed his heart, too. As he bid the guys goodbye and headed for home, Cayden's teasing wifey comment swirled in Desmond's mind. If he were married, having a baby wouldn't be a scandal. All he needed was a woman willing to play that role.

Desmond pulled into the garage with a loosely formed plan, one as potentially genius as it was insane. He'd undoubtedly have to pull on all of his charisma and employ all his sales, marketing and negotiating skills, but if successful, Ivy Campbell's job description was about to expand.

Nine

"Shh, it's okay, sweetie," Ivy cooed, bouncing a cranky Desiree on her hip as she crisscrossed the living space. "I'm frustrated, too."

And she was. She'd never done the nanny thing before so perhaps Desmond coming in too late to spend time with Desiree wasn't her business. Maybe texting her boss regarding his whereabouts and expected ETA had not been the right thing to do. But in the three days she'd been employed, Desmond hadn't spent three minutes with his daughter. Learning he'd never even held her had shocked her into the brash act of urging him home.

Ivy knew that with some people intimacy with one's child took time and could understand why that was the case with Desmond. She also knew how important it was for a child to bond with the parent, and how rejection and indifference could be felt from a very young age. She thought the connection would be as beneficial to Desmond, if not even more so. Any real time spent around this little girl and there was no choice but to fall in love. Not only was she a good baby for the most part, crying only when hungry, wet or having the rare bad day as she was right now, but she also couldn't have looked more like Desmond had he spit her out. Ivy didn't know what part in her looks the mother played, but as for Desmond, the child looked just like him.

At the same time the angel on one side touted these virtues and why it was important she advocate for the child, the devil on the other shoulder cautioned her involvement. How much say did a nanny have when it came to how a parent interacted with his child? She'd certainly heard of situations where children, in fact entire generations, were raised almost exclusively by the help or nuns or boarding school teachers. Was there any conclusive data to say that they'd been negatively impacted?

She reached for her pad to do some quick research but before she could pull up a search engine, she heard the garage door opening and Desmond's car being driven inside. Desiree's whimpers had somewhat subsided but when she prepared to lay her in the crib bed, the protests began again.

Ivy sighed and shifted her to the other hip as she walked toward the hall where Desmond would enter.

"Ivy," he called out from the hallway outside her suite.

"One moment!" And then to Desiree, "Okay, little one. Be on your best behavior. It's time to get to know your dad."

She crossed the living room and entered the hallway. Desmond loitered at the base of the stairs. She walked directly to him and with no forethought on how else to do it, thrust the baby in his arms.

"What the—"

"Can you hold her for a moment?"

Desmond was speechless, his eyes those of a deer in headlights. Ivy resisted the urge to chuckle and instead offered instruction as she boldly placed the child against Desmond's chest. He had no choice but to embrace her and did so as though the child were a UFO.

She gently pushed his arms inward so the child was snuggled against him. "That's it. Hold her close to your chest."

"I might drop her."

"There's nothing to fear. Your daughter is stronger than she looks. She trusts you, and so do I."

Desiree looked up at her dad, smiled, began cooing and kicking her legs.

"What is she doing?"

"If I didn't know better, I'd say she's letting you know how happy she is to be in your arms."

"I feel like an idiot."

"Why?"

"I don't know. This feels awkward."

"You've never held a baby?"

"To say I haven't sounds impossible, but honestly if I have, it's been so long ago that I can't remember."

"Would you like to sit down with her?"

"No."

Ivy couldn't help but laugh at that. "I appreciate the honest answer. But it's important for Desiree to know you—your smell, touch, voice, feel. Science and psychology experts have proven that the bond between fathers and daughters is more important than previously thought."

"I don't remember my dad holding me and I turned out okay."

"Are you sure about that?"

Ivy was as surprised at the sarcastic reaction as Desmond. They both laughed. The tension lessened.

"It would be great if you could hold her for just a few minutes."

"Okay."

"See, you automatically placed your hand behind her neck to support it. Looks like you're a natural."

"In this instance, flattery will get you everywhere. Plus, I need the encouragement so keep coming with the positive words."

They reached the sofa. Desmond slowly sat down. Ivy arranged Desiree more securely in the crook of his arm, then sat in a nearby chair. She was silent, her heart pleased as she watched Desmond gaze at his child.

"She's got my eyes," he said finally.

"And dimple," Ivy added.

"Mom and Dad call her Desi."

"I know."

"I guess I can see why, a little bit."

"I'd say a lot bit. Your mother showed me one of your baby pictures. The two of you could have been twins."

"Not a week in and Mom's already pulling out the family albums? Sounds like she and I need to have a conversation."

"Don't be too hard on her. She's an extremely proud grandmother and means you no harm."

"If only that could be said for everyone."

Desiree began fussing. Ivy reached for her quickly before Desmond freaked out. She tested the diaper. It was dry. She checked her watch.

"Almost time to feed her." She looked at Desmond. "Since you don't remember ever holding a baby, you've probably never held a bottle, either."

She headed out of the room toward the bottle holder in the nursery.

"Hey! Where are you going?"

"Be right back!"

Within minutes, Desiree was being fed by her father. At one point, she kicked and gave him a milky smile. Ivy swore she saw his heart melting.

"It's not all bad, huh?" At his questioning gaze, she added, "Being a dad."

"It's not the what, but the how. I'm still shocked and confused at how all of this went down."

"That's understandable."

"She's innocent and all, but Desi's arrival, it could cause a lot of problems."

"How so?"

"People talk. That's not good."

"A baby is nothing to be ashamed of."

"Technically true, but having yours delivered by courier is the type of news you don't want to see in print."

"Understood. Where's the mom?"

"We don't know."

"Why do you think she chose not to keep her?"

"I don't know that, either."

Ivy watched as a line of formula dribbled out of Desiree's mouth. "Looks like she's about to go to sleep," she said, walking over to dab Desiree's wet chin with a cloth. "Let's burp her so I can put her to bed."

Ivy explained the burping-baby process, placed the cloth over Desmond's left shoulder, then laid the baby there.

"That's right. Continue to pat her back softly, just like that."

Desmond awkwardly patted his daughter's back. "Are you sure this works?"

"Positive."

A few seconds later, Desiree burped. Desmond beamed. "Hey! I did it!"

"Yes you did, Daddy. All by yourself. I'd say this first

real interaction was successful. Would you like to put her to bed?"

Desmond shook his head. "The bottle and burping lessons are enough for one night."

Ivy gently pulled Desiree from Desmond's arms. "Alright, then, that will be lesson two. Thanks for stopping by." She reached the hall and turned back. "Perhaps you can spend some time with her each evening. That will help immensely in her getting to know you."

"I'm a busy man."

"I know. Nothing major, just a few minutes would be enough for now."

"I'll think about it."

"I appreciate it, Desmond." She shifted Desiree into her other arm. "This will take a minute. She needs to be given a light sponge bath and changed. Please let yourself out. Good night."

Ivy talked to Desiree while performing these duties. She didn't use baby talk, but spoke in clear, complete sentences.

"Did you enjoy spending time with your handsome daddy? You did? Yes? Wasn't too bad for a first-time feed, huh? He looked the part; smelled good, too. He'll be an old pro in no time."

Once Desiree was ensconced in her canopied crib, Ivy returned to the living room and was met with a surprise.

"You're still here?"

Desmond's expression was neutral. "I am."

Oh, no! Did he hear my comments about him being handsome and smelling good? Ivy was all smiles and calm on the outside but really wanted to make like a friendly ghost and disappear. She walked over and took a seat across from Desmond.

"Um, did you hear me talking to Desiree?"

"You talked to her as though she could understand you."

Ivy's heartbeat increased. "Did you hear what I told her?"

"I wasn't paying much attention. Why, were you sharing state secrets that only my daughter can know?"

"Something like that." Ivy visibly relaxed. "You need to speak with me about something?"

Desmond leaned back against the couch. "What would you do?"

"About what?"

"Finding a baby on your doorstep. Being in my shoes."

Ivy pondered the question as she sat back down. "I'd handle it the way I do all other challenges. Break the situation down into manageable steps and then take appropriate action."

"That would be easy if I knew the steps."

"One day at a time. You'll figure it out."

"You're a smart, educated woman. Can you help me?"

"Me?"

"Sure, why not? I don't have a clue where to begin."

Ivy rose from her chair and paced the room. After a few seconds, she stopped. "What is the number one problem created by Desiree's presence?"

"Her presence is the problem. We are a high-profile family, as you know. We pride ourselves on maintaining a stellar reputation, both personally and professionally. Even though it's the twenty-first century, we hold on to a few traditional values. Like being married before having children, and making sure our offspring carry on all that comes with being a part of the Eddington clan."

Ivy sat back down with a serious look. "Then it sounds like there's only one solution. Marry her mother."

"The one who lied, connived and committed the ultimate betrayal?"

"People don't always marry for love."

"Other than co-parenting, I want nothing to do with Desiree's mother." Desmond paused, looked at her oddly. "But you could be right. Getting married could be a step in preventing a scandal and fixing this…situation."

"A marriage of convenience," Ivy replied, feeling helpful. "Happens all the time."

"I'd just have to find the person willing to do it, understand it's a business arrangement and play by the rules."

"Do you know someone like that who'd be willing to help you?"

"Perhaps," Desmond said, his gaze intensifying. "Ivy Campbell, will you marry me?"

Ten

It was as though Ivy had entered the twilight zone. *Did that man just say what I think he said?*

"You're kidding, right?" she asked, after grabbing sodas for each of them and a bowl of nuts.

"Obviously, having this job is helping you move on from a tragic situation, right? Agreeing to this would be helping me out of an unfortunate one. We could help each other. Financially, I'd make it more than worth your while."

Too stunned to formulate an appropriate comeback, Ivy sipped her soda instead.

"It's probably not the kind of proposal that little girls dream of but, Ivy, this situation could be a win-win."

The statement was so incredulous it unstuck Ivy's tongue. "How do you figure?"

"You want to start a girl's school, correct?"

"Yes." Her nod, slow, the response, delayed.

"What if in exchange for a marriage of convenience, I agreed to help fund your school?"

"This is crazy. I don't even know why we're talking about it."

"Because it's a possible solution, that's why." This time it was Desmond who stood and paced.

"You already live here and are taking care of Desiree. We could find a place with lax laws to marry, preferably out of the country, wait a few months until we've settled into the situation, and then issue a short press release about falling in love at first sight or some equally romantic story you women are into, and announce that we married while on vacation."

"A destination wedding."

"Is that what they call them? Yeah, we could announce that it was something like that."

"You're really serious?"

"Hey, this was your idea."

"I couldn't do that, Desmond."

"Why not?"

"First of all, as my employer, even the suggestion is in-appropriate. Secondly, what am I supposed to do with my emotions or even more importantly, my life? Am I to raise your daughter, live with someone for whom there is a mutually agreed upon business arrangement but no love, and then, oh, in about eighteen years, once Desiree is grown and attending college, quietly get a divorce from you and try and pick up my life? Let's see, I'm twenty-seven now so by then I'll be forty-five, already over the age of safe childbearing for the child of my own I might want to have. Would there be a contractual clause for you to pay for my IVF rounds, if needed, along with funding my school?"

For the first time since the asinine conversation started, Desmond's eyes flickered with uncertainty.

He shrugged. "We could probably work something out."

"I'm sure there's someone out there who'd jump at the chance to take your money. But that's not me."

"Are you sure? We haven't even talked numbers."

"We don't need to. This makes no sense."

"How much would you need to get your school started?"

Ivy didn't hesitate in providing the answer. Formulating a business plan had been a part of the program for her master's degree.

"Two million."

"I'd give you four."

Ivy had been about to take a drink. Her hand stopped midway to her mouth. "Four million dollars?"

"Cash."

"How long would this ruse have to last? Some nannies stay with children until they are grown."

Desmond shrugged. "Once the baby news dies down and someone else grabs the headlines, we could quietly divorce."

"So we'd go from faking a marriage to putting your daughter through the trauma of divorce."

"You could continue on as her nanny until whatever age you feel she could handle the change."

Her look conveyed the annoyance she felt. Were they really having this conversation?

"What about me? My life? My feelings? And what about you? What about dating? What happens when you fall in love for real?"

"I could build a new home with separate wings, or build an adjoining residence. Or perhaps I could announce that a marriage took place without it even happening. Hey, that's an even better idea, one without any legal ramifications. You could pose as my wife for a number of years and then once my dad secures the position for which he's being considered and our business remains solid, we can go our own ways and live our own lives, simple as that."

"Simple, huh?"

"It can be."

"Doesn't sound like it, especially if your dad is thinking about running for president."

"Not of the country, at least not yet. He is campaigning to become president of the Society."

"What Society?"

"The Society of Ma'at."

"Never heard of it."

"Are you serious?"

"I'm not into corporate business."

"The Society of Ma'at is a professional organization, a fraternity of sorts, that affects every area of life all over the globe."

"Sounds prestigious."

"Very. That's why preventing a scandal right now is extremely important. Tell me you'll at least think about it?"

"Desmond, really, there's nothing to think about. As a woman of character and integrity, this proposal is impossible, even borderline insulting. It's not something I'd consider."

"Even for four million dollars?"

"Even so."

"How about eight?"

It took Ivy longer to answer this time. "Even for eight."

She held his gaze and maintained her composure, but her response held a certainty that neither her head nor heart felt.

The next morning, Ivy awoke from a restless, troubled sleep as stunned as she had been last night. She performed her morning ablutions and dressed in a fog. Had Desmond really asked her to marry him? Had their subsequent discussion about such a ridiculous question been for real? But for seeing Desiree's bottle on the table next to where Desmond had fed her, she would have sworn she'd dreamed the visit. The more she remembered about last night, the more she knew for sure that she hadn't been dreaming. Both the visit and Desmond's marriage proposal had been all too real.

Ivy Campbell, will you marry me?

You're kidding, right?

Just hear me out…

Ivy opened her tablet and logged into her email, trying to enjoy the quiet before Desiree awakened and to focus on something, anything, besides the child's father. Not possible. Visions of his face kept swimming before her eyes, how as he'd laid out the "business proposition" his expression had gone from worried to hopeful. The more he'd warmed up to the idea, the colder she'd felt. Yes, she was the one who'd suggested marriage. But to Shelly, the child's mother, not her. If not, surely there was some free and fancy socialite wanting to come up, a woman for whom a marriage to someone like Desmond would be mutually beneficial. Given her physical response whenever that man neared her, and the flights of fancy she'd refused to entertain on other occasions, a marriage of convenience to Desmond would be akin to moving into heartbreak hotel.

Having this job is helping you move on from a tragic situation, right? Agreeing to this would be helping me out of an unfortunate one. We could help each other. Financially, I'd make it more than worth your while.

The more she recalled the conversation, the angrier she got. How dare he treat marriage like a business proposition! He'd been as comfortable explaining the plan as he had been in hiring her as a nanny, as though this asinine idea was just another job offer. Didn't she realize he was asking her to officially put her life on hold through her childbearing years, not to mention live a lie in the process? Did he not understand that most women couldn't set their hearts aside and let their heads lead when it came to relationships, even a fake one? Did all rich people think money was the end all be all answer to every problem, and that one could buy themselves out of whatever trouble they found themselves in? What was she supposed to do about those pesky little creatures like feelings and emotions? What would happen if she actually fell in love?

Ivy knew that answer. Pain, that's what.

Even knowing what he'd asked was impractical, improbable and should never ever happen, Ivy found herself replaying the conversation again and again. As morning gave way to afternoon, she began second-guessing the practicality of dismissing Desmond's suggestion outright. He had, in fact, made her an offer that was hard—if not impossible—to refuse.

It's times like these that she wished she'd spent more time cultivating female friendships. She'd met Gerald when a freshman in college. They'd become both a couple and each other's best friend. Knowing his practicality, which matched her own, he'd probably tell her to go for it. Just like a man. To work this out, Ivy needed a woman's perspective. Talking to Lynn was out of the question, which left one other person. Her mother, Helen. In the weeks since taking the job, Ivy hadn't returned to Helen's apartment. Their phone calls were infrequent. This particular situation warranted a visit. Ivy prepared Desiree's diaper bag, left a message with Bernice that she and the baby would be out for a couple hours, then got in her car and headed to Chicago for a visit with her mom.

Eleven

Desmond stopped by his parents' home on the way to the office. He knew they'd be in the solarium, Mona's favorite place, and headed straight there. He skipped civil greetings and pleasantries and got straight to the point of his visit.

"I may have come up with a way to solve this baby mess."

Derrick and Mona, in the process of enjoying their preferred morning beverages, looked up as their mugs hung in midair.

"I take issue with you calling my darling grandchild a *mess*," Mona said, before adding, "And good morning to you, too."

"Good morning, Mom." He walked over and kissed the cheek she offered, then gave Derrick a nod. "Dad."

"Son," Derrick answered around another sip of coffee before setting down the cup. "Whatever you call this situation, it's one that needs a solution, pronto. If you've got one, Desmond, I'm all ears."

"Before I get to that, what did Bob want?"

"To tell me that my chances for the presidency were looking good and to remind me of how what happened with Cayden last year had almost cost him the membership. I told him that he had nothing to worry about and felt like a lying ass the whole time."

"Then my solution is surely to make you feel better." He steeled himself for the declaration. "I can get married."

Mona almost choked on the tea she'd just sipped, and reached for a napkin to blot the droplets before they stained her haute couture sweater.

Derrick, however, was laser focused. "They've located Shelly?"

"No."

Mona chuckled softly. "Hard to pull off a wedding without a bride."

"I can marry the nanny, Ivy. Strictly a business arrangement, of course." Desmond sat and continued amid his parent's shocked silence. "We could agree to a partnership of, say, five years or so, until the child is older, and any speculation of her sudden appearance dies down. Then we can quietly divorce and go on with our individual, personal lives."

Derrick steepled his fingers. "You've discussed this with Ivy?"

"Yes."

"And she's agreed?" Mona asked.

"Not exactly."

"You might want to get that agreement before thinking this solution—" Mona used air quotes "—is a viable one. From the short time I've known her, she doesn't appear to be one who can be easily bought."

Desmond knew from last night's convo that his mother spoke the gospel truth.

"I did make an offer and yes, she refused, but in time I think her firm no can be turned into a more pliable yes."

"How?" Derrick asked.

"You know she wants to start a girl's school."

Mona nodded. "We talked about that."

"I offered her between four and eight million dollars. With that money she'd be financially independent and in a position to realize her dream."

"You know, Des, it sounds crazy but that plan has teeth. As an educational endeavor, some of that money could come through our nonprofit. She wasn't open to that idea at all?"

"She wasn't last night," Desmond responded, remembering how she described being offended. "But she's had a night to sleep on it. Today's another day."

Mona shifted to face her son fully. "What happens if and when Shelly returns and wants to reclaim her daughter, which until legal documents are signed or a certain amount of time passes she could absolutely do? What then happens to the sham of a marriage you created to uphold the Eddington legacy and legitimize Desiree? As importantly, what happens to Ivy if she's unable to maintain this business relationship—" air quotes again "—and falls in love?

"Most importantly, what happens when Shelly plays the mama card to become Mrs. Desmond Eddington?"

"Shelly's not like that."

"Before that fateful Friday, you probably didn't think she was like the kind of woman who'd leave a baby with the guard."

Derrick and Mona had given Desmond a lot to think about. Before leaving his father had reiterated how important it was to locate Shelly and get her to sign the NDA. His parents weren't as worried about her telling the truth as they were of her creating a story that made her look like the jilted lover and their grandchild like a baby Desmond did not want. He left their house and headed to work more unsettled than when he'd arrived, with more questions than answers and more uncertainty than confidence.

Fortunately, as chaotic as Desmond found his personal life, professionally, business was booming. A group of African billionaires had formed a consortium and together purchased a billion-dollar block of E-Squared Crypto. The market exploded. Media swarmed. In the financial world, Desmond's profile rose to new heights. Overnight, he became one of the leading experts in digital currency and was courted by all the major news outlets to appear on their shows. It brought all kinds of people out of the woodwork, including every woman he'd ever dated, almost everyone he'd ever met. Even Penelope forgave him and offered a standing invitation to Paris or wherever she was in the world. They had a pleasant conversation, so much so that Desmond considered asking her about getting married as a business arrangement. That lasted for an entire nanosecond. Penelope was a driven, power-seeking, shrewd-thinking woman. If she ever got a legal claw in him, she'd never let go.

For the next two weeks, the whirl of activity put aside thoughts of marriage, finding Shelly and everything else. He worked twelve-hour days and spent his evenings networking and hobnobbing with some of the richest, most powerful people in the world. Communication between him and Ivy was largely reduced to brief phone calls and text messages. Visits with his daughter were rare, a fact for which tonight his mother had chided him. She spent a lot of time with her granddaughter and spoke frequently with Ivy as a result.

"She's really amazing with Desi," her mom told him.

"And I agree with her that you should make more time for your child."

"How often am I the topic of your conversation?" he'd asked her.

Mona hadn't answered his question. Instead, she offered advice. "They grow up fast, Desmond. One minute you're pregnant, the next the child is graduating high school. Those early years are precious and they're ones you don't get back."

Desmond hadn't said much after that but his mother's words had hit a mark. When he got home that night, he decided to go down and kiss his child good-night. It was after one in the morning. He had no doubt that both the child and her nanny would be fast asleep. He crept downstairs, eased down the hall and gently pushed wider a door that was already ajar. That's when he got a view that was totally unexpected. Ivy's perfect, upturned, delicious-looking ass leaning over to place Desiree in the crib. Something in his brain told him to turn away and back out of the room but he was mesmerized, paralyzed, unable to move. Ivy dressed conservatively, but nothing short of a burlap bag would have hidden the curves he'd imagined. Now what he'd believed to be under her loose-fitting clothing was on full display, causing him to harden on the spot. Before he could do the right thing and make a hasty exit, she turned around.

"Ah!"

One hand flew to the perky breasts barely concealed behind a strappy top. The other grabbed a stuffed animal and placed it over the matching lacy triangle covering her treasure.

"Desmond!" Her voice was high-pitched and breathless.

"Sorry." Finally, he found the wherewithal to avert his gaze. "Um, I came to see the baby."

"She's asleep."

Desmond didn't have to be looking to know that the answer had come through gritted teeth. He risked a glance in her direction. The pussycat toy had been replaced by one of Desiree's blankets. His normally rational mind had been replaced by that of a stranger's. It's the only explanation for what he said next.

"Have you given any more thought to that marriage offer?"

"Get. Out!"

"Right. I, uh, good night." With hands raised as though caught in the act of committing a crime, Desmond backed out of the room and headed up the stairs, mentally kicking himself for making such a rookie move. He was a pro with the ladies, had been perfecting his romance game since the tender age of thirteen. Of all the things he could have thought to say to her, what in the world had possessed him to ask that question? Sleep deprivation. That had to be it. He'd been burning the candle at both ends for the past couple weeks. Obviously, it had muddled his brain.

He didn't get much sleep that night. The next day's schedule was packed full beginning with a breakfast meeting and ending with a social event that wouldn't see him home until midnight. There were eight- and nine-figure deals on his desk waiting for his perusal and input. But the only thing on his mind was a smooth brown round moon of a pair of buttocks that had etched themselves into his visual memory and had him wanting to cop a feel, and more. During the short drive to work, he came up with a plan and was glad that Janice was already working at her desk.

"Good morning, Janice."

"Good morning, Desmond. Don't you look dapper today."

Desmond smiled at the throwback word. "Thanks. You always look nice."

"I try."

"I've got meetings back-to-back all day but need something handled. Can you help?"

"Of course."

Desmond left instructions that involved a floral shop, a high-end jeweler and a call to a friend to see if there was an extra ticket for tonight's private show he'd been invited to attend. His family always treated their employees well. He tried to convince himself that this was just another example of that high-end treatment. But deep inside, he knew that it wasn't. There was something attractive about Ivy Campbell that had nothing to do with her work as a nanny, and everything to do with the beautiful woman he was discovering her to be…both inside and out.

Twelve

He saw my bare ass!

All morning, try as she might, what happened in the wee hours of the morning was the only thing Ivy could think about. Everything had happened so quickly it almost felt like a dream. Almost being the operative word. Both Ivy's head and heart told her that what took place had been all too real. The way her heart had pounded when she turned and saw him. What appeared to her to be a look of desire in his hooded eyes. The goose bumps that broke out at the very thought that he could want her. The embarrassment that was undoubtedly felt by them both.

His unexpected appearance left Ivy with questions, not to mention put a whole other spin on her conversation with Mom. To get the questions answered required a conversation with Desmond. The thought of talking to him, let alone seeing him, filled her with dread. Remembering that look in his eyes before he turned away caused a wave of excitement to burst through caution and wash over her. She tried to ignore the message her body conveyed. She was more than a little attracted to her boss. A part of her wanted to see his ass, too. Which is why the conversation she'd had with her mom was on her mind, the one where she sounded less like the woman who lived life spontaneously and more like Ivy who lived life in black-and-white. It wasn't often that Helen Campbell said something that Ivy agreed with, let alone took a position where Ivy could be swayed to her side. But Ivy was a practical sort who weighed situations objectively, without emotion. And what her mother had said during their visit weeks ago made a whole lot of sense.

"Hey, Mom."

Helen looked up from the television show she was watching. "About time you came to check on me."

Ivy refused to be baited into an argument. "We've talked," she said instead. "I've been busy. You remember the time needed caring for a newborn, right?"

Helen tsked. "I took care of you while working a full-time job and going to nursing school. With a babysitter, not a nanny. So let's not talk busy, okay?"

"I don't see how you did it." Ivy moved various items from a cushion of what had become a catchall couch and sat down.

"Wasn't easy." Helen shifted in her chair and changed the channel. "So how is it trying to keep up with the Joneses?"

"There's no keeping up with the people in the Point. I stay in my lane as a child's nanny." *Liar!* "Which given what a sweet baby she is, really isn't that hard."

She shared a bit more about Desiree, while making sure not to mention Desmond or the Eddington name. The whole NDA situation actually helped her not have to reveal too much. She grabbed a pillow and watched TV for a while, though later if asked, she wouldn't have been able to describe the show. Her thoughts were on Desmond and marriages of convenience, and on the father that she and her mother rarely discussed. Finally, figuring there was no easy way to start a hard conversation, she jumped into the middle.

"Mom, I know we don't often discuss it, but did you love Dad?"

"What kind of cockamamie question is that?"

"Well, I'm sure you loved him but were you in love with him?"

"What difference does it make?"

Gerald came to mind. With a modicum of guilt, Ivy deflected any potential questions about her employer by centering the conversation around the deceased.

"I don't know," she said with a shrug, working to keep her voice casual. "I miss Gerald, but in thinking about what we had, I realize we were great friends and I loved him but I'm not sure we were ever in love."

Her mother tsked. "Don't let those Hallmark movies fool you. Real love in real life doesn't look like that."

"So, you weren't in love with Daddy?"

"I loved Ralph. Respected him. I was young, broke, needed a place to stay. He was a hard worker, lonely, wanted companionship. We had our own reasons for tying the knot but loved each other well enough. If he hadn't died of a heart attack, we'd probably still be married."

Helen's eyes moved from the TV screen to her daughter. "Why all these questions? You met somebody?"

Ivy shook her head. "No, not really."

"Well, you need to. I know you've suffered a huge tragedy with Gerald getting killed and all, but you've still got a lot of life ahead of you. Don't spend it alone."

"I don't want to."

"And don't get another boyfriend from that uppity crowd. Stay in your place. Gerald was a nice enough young man but his parents were as fake as a twenty dollar Louis Vuitton."

Ivy didn't dare comment. If her mother knew everything that had gone down with her would-be in-laws, and the actions that had forced her to flee Atlanta, there would be no stopping a confrontation. Helen wasn't afraid of anybody and she suffered no fools.

"I all but told her that when she called here the other day."

Ivy froze. "Who?"

"Gerald's phony mama, Bonnie."

Ivy's world tilted on its axis. She thought leaving Atlanta would put an end to the Russell family drama, that and the official police report stating that the accident that night had not been her fault. She'd waived her rights to anything belonging to Gerald, including those items they'd purchased together. He'd placed her on his life insurance policy. She'd signed that over to his parents as well. She'd abandoned her studies in the city she loved. She'd left their state. What more did they want from her?

"When did this happen?"

Helen gave a dispassionate wave of the hand. "A week or so ago."

"And you didn't tell me?"

"I'd forgotten about it, to be honest."

Ivy took a calming breath. Helen knew nothing of what had transpired between her and Gerald's family. Ivy planned to keep it that way.

"Did she say what she wanted?"

"Only that she'd tried to reach you, but your number had changed."

"That was it?"

"Pretty much. She asked if I knew how to get in touch with you and I told her of course I did. You're my daughter! But I also told her that you didn't live here anymore, that you weren't in Chicago."

Helen gave Ivy a conspiratorial look. "That's technically true."

"Thanks, Mom."

"Now, you want to tell me why you looked like a deer in headlights just now when I told you that news?"

"It just…surprised me, that's all. Bonnie and Gerald Sr. never accepted me. They didn't think I was good enough for their son. Now that he's gone, I've cut all ties with Atlanta. I never want to hear from or talk to them again."

Her heart back to its regular beat, Ivy changed the subject. "Enough about me and my life, Mom. I'm worried about you."

"Don't you start on me with that healthy eating mess. Your uncle Charlie lived to be ninety-one and he drank beer and ate ballpark franks covered in mustard and jalapeño peppers until the day he died."

"I wasn't going to talk about that, though your diet and apparent shopping addiction do concern me. I'm talking about you finding companionship, maybe falling love again."

"I am in love."

Ivy's eyes lit up. "That's excellent, Mom! Who with?"

"Idris Elba. He's the best kind of husband, one I can watch when I want to and turn him off when need be."

Ivy visited with her mom for another two hours and enjoyed the best time with her that she'd had in a while. When she left, she was no closer to making a decision about Desmond's offer but instead of the fast no that she'd initially given, she was more open to a slow yes. She tried to block out the unexpected news of Bonnie's phone call but she couldn't deny her fear. All she kept hearing were the last words delivered in their final conversation.

You took my son's life and caused a lifetime of suffering. We will work to return the favor.

* * *

What a dilemma. What would she do about the Russells trying to find her? Should she share any of what went on with Desmond, and if so, how much? He knew about the accident. He didn't know she'd been driving or that Gerald's parents blamed her for his death. They'd all but painted her as a murderer. If they crossed paths, which wasn't totally unlikely, would Desmond believe them? Especially if provided details she hadn't willingly shared, ones that hadn't come up during the background check?

Then there was the matter of Desiree. She provided a much-needed spark in Ivy's attempt to fire back up her life. Thoughts of Desmond brought on a whole other kind of heat. But Ivy wasn't interested in love. Plus, he wasn't her type. And she definitely wasn't the type of woman he dated. Thoughts of being intimate with Desmond were not only inappropriate, but as likely to happen as was the chance she'd fly to the moon. Or marry for money instead of love, even with her dream of a school thrown into the bargain. They hadn't spoken about that arrangement since that initial conversation. That he'd brought it up as she stood half naked further soured her on the idea of it being a workable solution. Clearly, he expected sex to be a part of the deal.

The doorbell rang. She was glad for the rare and unexpected interruption. She walked to the door, peered out the side panel and was taken aback at a large bouquet of gigantic roses that hid the deliveryman's face. That didn't deter her from answering the door. The Eddington Estate was like a fortress. She felt safer here than anywhere in the world.

Once the door opened, Ivy realized the man wasn't actually carrying the flowers. The arrangement was much too large for that. It sat on a flat delivery cart, the handle of which the man firmly grasped as he offered a bright smile.

"Hello."

"Good morning, miss!"

"You know what, most deliveries allowed through are dropped off at the side door but for that one I should probably let you in upstairs so they can be left in the foyer."

His smile faltered a bit. "Those weren't my instructions."

He checked his cell phone. "Yes, I'm at the right door. These are for you."

"Me? Are you sure?"

"Are you Ivy Campbell?"

"Yes."

The man nodded. "These come compliments of one Mr. Desmond Eddington. The vase is extremely heavy. If you'll allow me inside, I can place it wherever you'd like."

Stunned speechless, Ivy stepped back so the man could enter. As he wheeled the cart past her, she caught the pungent aroma. She had to give it Desmond. When the man apologized, he did it first-class.

"Wow. This home is as spectacular as is this arrangement. Where would you like this set?"

She looked around. "Here is fine."

Using a type of lifting crane on the cart Ivy hadn't noticed, the vase was placed on the downstairs foyer's marble floor.

"You'll want to be careful with this piece, ma'am. It's a Japanese Imari. Collector's item. Something you'll want to save and pass on to your children. The longer you have them, the greater the value. But don't worry, Mr. Eddington took care of having it fully insured."

He insured a vase? How expensive was it?

"Those roses are something special, too. Grown only in the mountains of Ecuador."

"I've never seen a more beautiful flower. They look fake, and I can't believe the smell is so strong."

"Yep, and that ain't no spray neither. Au naturel for sure. Our shop only services high-end clients with product flown in daily from all over the world."

His phone beeped.

"Well, that's it, ma'am. Got to get to the next client."

"Of course. Let me get your tip."

"Already taken care of, ma'am. Enjoy those beautiful flowers. Have a nice day!"

Ivy walked the man to the door, then went back to admire the floral arrangement that almost came up to her five foot five. The fragrance enveloped her. The myriad of colors was unnaturally bright, some tinted bicolor. Bright oranges faded into soft yellow. Lavender roses tinged in deep purple. Other colors—hot pink, red, mint green, blue—a profusion of beauty unlike she'd ever seen. The softest petals she'd ever touched. She walked to the other side, still enthralled. Tucked near the bottom of one of the groupings was an envelope. She plucked it out and pulled out a card. On one side, in beautiful calligraphy were two words.

I'm sorry.

On the other side, an invitation.

Please join me for an apology I'm sure you'll enjoy.

Before Ivy could process the message, her cell phone rang. An unknown number. She usually didn't answer unidentified callers, but she didn't usually get bouquets five-feet high.

"Hello."

"Hi, Ivy?"

"Yes."

"My name is Janice. I'm Desmond's secretary. He's in back-to-back meetings and asked that I call you regarding tonight's event."

"What kind of event?"

"He didn't provide many details, but I do know it's

formal. He asked that I arrange for a stylist to assist your preparation. A car will be by to pick you up promptly at seven. The stylists will arrive at four."

"Look, I probably should speak to Desmond. He knows I can't meet him. I have a baby…" Ivy's hand flew to her mouth. *Dammit, I just violated the NDA!* The four words she'd uttered could cost her not only her job but several thousand dollars if Desmond decided to sue.

"Desmond explained that you'd need a babysitter. He says that you know Bernice's granddaughter, Sabrina. She'll be by this afternoon to pick up your child."

Your child. Those words produced an unexpected pang in Ivy's chest. She and Gerald had never talked much about family. But Ivy always envisioned a child or two in her future.

"This is…I don't…is there any way I can speak with him really quickly?"

"I'm afraid not, Ivy. He's in a series of very important meetings and cannot be disturbed. He told me that you might put up resistance and if that happened, to advise you that your attendance is mandatory. He'll be waiting in the lobby. Should you have any questions between now and then, please don't hesitate to call me. I'll text you my direct number. The stylists will see you at four. Have fun!"

Fun. Ivy couldn't remember the last time that word had actually applied to her life. She'd never been much of a partier and thankfully neither was Gerald. Another thing they had in common. Dinner and a movie was their idea of a night on the town. And what in the heck did she have in her closet that could be styled? She was familiar with the concept. Knew that the looks celebrities modeled on the red carpet were often put together by professionals using designer duds. Ivy didn't have anything she thought would pass for formal attire. Still, she trudged down the hall to the closet to see if there was anything there that would help the stylist create a miracle.

She'd almost exhausted all possible options, none of them good, when the doorbell rang. Again? This time it was Sabrina, there to pick up Desiree.

"I know I'm early," she said after they'd shared greetings. "But Miss Mona told me to get Desiree and bring her up to the house. Her board meeting got canceled so she's free this afternoon."

The rest of the time went by in a blur. Not one but a team of stylists showed up at her front door with everything a woman needed to go from looking like a stepchild to being the princess at the ball. One of the stylists literally wheeled in a clothing rack full of evening gown choices in a variety of sizes. Another brought in a container of designer shoes and a carry-on bag filled with jewelry. She was picked, plucked and pampered from head to toe, given a French mani-pedi and against her better judgment was talked into having extensions added to her shoulder-length flat-ironed hair. When she stood in front of her full-length floor mirror, she marveled at what had happened to Ivy Campbell and had no idea who the woman was staring back at her. When the driver arrived and escorted her to a gleaming platinum-colored Mercedes-Maybach limo, the fantasy was complete. Ivy officially felt like Cinderella. However, her mother's news about Bonnie calling and dating advice came back to haunt her.

Don't get with that uppity crowd. Stay in your place.

Ivy forced away the thoughts and tried to retrieve her former excitement. She only hoped the evening wouldn't end with her turning into a pumpkin and the beautiful clothes she wore becoming rags.

Thirteen

Desmond stifled a yawn and tried to look interested as a billionaire from Kentucky went on and on about his state-of-the-art, top-of-the-line horse breeding and training facility. All the while, he kept up surreptitious surveillance of the Point du Sable Country Club's front door. Janice had told him how hesitant Ivy sounded to accept the invitation. Even though he'd described her attendance as mandatory, as happy hour wound down and it got closer to showtime, Desmond wasn't sure she would show up. The lobby was crowded, filled with designer this and sparkling that covering beauty and handsomeness. A few of his past friends with benefits flitted through the crowd, some with their now husbands or fiancés. Still more hopefuls slid him coy, seductive glances, while other bolder types insinuated themselves into the quartet of men chatting to flirt or say hello. Clearly, he had no idea what a Ms. Magnet he was in the tux he'd changed into before leaving the office. The charcoal gray one-button style fit to perfection, showing off a perfectly toned six-foot-plus bod. Those who knew him wouldn't describe Desmond as metrosexual but he prided himself on meticulous grooming, as evidenced by his expertly lined hair, flawless skin courtesy of charcoal facials and good genes, and trimmed, manicured nails. The five-o'clock stubble added a roguish quality. It could be argued that the Eddington men were some of the handsomest in the room.

His thoughts were interrupted by a tap on the shoulder. "Where's your girl?"

"On her way," Desmond told Reign, with more confidence than he felt. His little sister hadn't been at the interview and was anxious to meet Ivy.

He'd told his siblings what a great job Ivy was doing with his daughter and to thank her she'd be joining them tonight. Maeve simply raised an eyebrow. Reign shrugged and went back to her full-time occupation, texting on her phone. Surprisingly, his jokester of a brother didn't tease him about it or ask for more details.

"Where's Tabitha?"

"Trying to worm her way into Maeve and Reign's good graces," Jake said. "Women ought to learn how to not try so hard to become someone's wife."

Desmond looked beyond Jake's shoulder. "That same lesson needs to be taught to Cornelius. He's following Maeve around like a dog after a bone."

"Cornelius is goofy but he's smart, successful, a solid guy. Maeve should quit playing around and marry the man."

"Guess she's following your advice about not trying too hard."

"You would be the one to use my words... Whoa! Who. Is. That?"

This time it was Desmond following Jake's gaze toward the front of the lobby. Later, he would have sworn that his heart skipped a beat, something he thought only happened in romance novels or chick flicks. Ivy was more beautiful than he'd imagined, surely more gorgeous than she believed.

Jake nudged him. "Do you know her?"

"Yes," Desmond said, a subtle smile spreading through him as his legs moved of their own accord. "That's my nanny."

"That's Ivy?" Jake asked incredulously. But Desmond didn't hear him. He was already halfway across the room.

He sidled up to her at the coat-check counter. "Hello, beautiful."

Her head whipped around. "Oh, Desmond. Thank goodness. I hoped to see you as soon as I arrived. I only came because Janice said this was mandatory, a part of my job. But I'm not staying."

"Why not?"

"I don't belong here."

"You belong here as much as anyone else. You truly do look amazing by the way. Jake saw you and didn't recognize you."

"I looked in the mirror and didn't recognize me, either."

The couple in front of her finished checking their coats and stepped away. "Miss, your coat, please."

"That's okay. I'm not…"

Desmond hooked his fingers around the collar of the faux chinchilla cape the stylist had paired perfectly with the stretch satin halter number in shimmering silver that hugged Ivy like they were in love.

"Desmond, look, you don't have to do this. The incredible bouquet was apology enough."

Ignoring her protests, he handed her wrap over to the clerk, pocketed the ticket and reached for her hand.

"Come with me. I want Mom and Dad to see your transformation."

"Only if you slow down. I can barely walk in these stilts they call heels."

Desmond was über-aware of the eyes that followed them across the lobby, a mixture of curiosity, jealousy and petty attitude. He hoped Ivy wouldn't be affected.

Mona looked up as they neared her. "Ivy, darling," she began with air kisses on both sides of Ivy's cheeks. "Glad you made it. You look amazing."

Desmond beamed. "See, I told you."

"Good evening, young lady," Derrick said, taking Ivy's hand and raising it to his lips for a gentlemanly kiss. "We're so glad you could join us. You're in for a special night."

As if on cue the sound of bells signaled the end of social hour. Time to move into the main ballroom.

"What is this event?" Ivy asked.

"You'll see."

The ballroom had been transformed into an intimate setting for a concert in the round. A gleaming grand piano sat in the center of a circular stage. Ambient lighting created a romantic mood. Desmond gave discreet greetings to a few of his friends as he led them to a front row seat with Jake and his date on one side and Maeve and Cornelius on the other. Only then did he give Ivy a copy of the exclusive linen invitation that had been sent to only three hundred lucky guests. On it was listed the night's up-close-and-personal entertainment—John Legend and Alicia Keys.

"They're really going to be here?" Ivy asked, unable to grasp that she was sitting this close to two of her favorite artists. "Not a talented pianist covering their songs?"

"Not a cover artist. We'll get to enjoy the real deal."

"How did you guys manage to get them to come here? They play in arenas with thousands of people."

"Good question. One you can ask when we meet them after the show."

His heart swelled as those beautiful lips he'd admired from their first meeting broke out into a huge smile, and her brown eyes twinkled. He took her arm, gently leading her into the ballroom, wanting to put that type of glow on her face in a myriad of different ways.

Ivy could really pinch herself this time. She had to be dreaming. The evening was one she could have never imagined in a world that she thought existed only on TV. For almost two hours, she'd been mere feet away from iconic talents, two of her favorites—how had he known?— and witnessed the best musical performances of her life. The last concert she'd attended was in Atlanta with Gerald at the Fox Theatre. For her birthday, he'd secured center seats in the lower balcony with unobstructed views of the Black Eyed Peas performing onstage. The evening had been exciting and memorable. But nothing like this. After the concert, a group even more exclusive than the three hundred attendees blessed to have witnessed such an awe-inspiring performance were able to spend an hour up close and personal with the celebrities backstage. Ivy was able to immortalize the evening and prove to future doubters that she hadn't hallucinated the whole thing— amazing selfies with both Alicia and John.

Once inside the arena-styled ballroom, Ivy's nerves had calmed. She'd noticed a few women cut their eyes in her direction, had seen two women with their heads together peering at her and whispering, no doubt wondering who was the woman with one of the most eligible bachelors in Point du Sable. One of those women provided the only truly awkward moment of the evening. As she stood near the entrance while Desmond went to the valet to have his car retrieved, she relived the interaction that took place between acts.

"Ah, man," Ivy heard Jake mumble as a beautiful woman in a bold winter-white Carly Cushnie original sauntered over and took the chair vacated when Jake's date excused herself to the restroom. "Here comes trouble."

Desmond said nothing at the woman's sugary greeting, but Ivy noted the crease that formed in his brow when she leaned down to place a kiss on his cheek before sitting down and directing her attention to Ivy.

"Hi. I don't believe we've met." She stuck out her hand. "Brittany Smith."

"Ivy Campbell." Said while noting the limp handshake, cold hand and even colder smile that didn't quite reach Brittany's eyes.

"Are you new to the area? I haven't seen you around."

"Probably because she minds her own business," Desmond responded. "Unlike some people I know."

"I used to date a friend of his so he doesn't trust me," Brittany said with a wink, tapping Ivy's leg as though they were old friends. "My motives are completely harmless. Like I said, I don't remember seeing you before and wanted to welcome you to the club."

Jake stood abruptly. "Man, I'm going to the bar. You want anything?"

Desmond shook his head. "No, bro, I'm good."

"What about you, Ivy?"

"No, thank you."

That he didn't extend the question to Brittany was a slight that seemed not to have registered. She watched

Jake walk up the aisle and then returned her attention to Desmond.

"Did you hear the news?"

"What news?"

She extended her arm across Ivy and wriggled her fingers to highlight a Flintstone-sized diamond on the fourth finger of her left hand.

"Lawrence and I are getting married."

"Congratulations." Said with about as much genuineness as reality TV.

"Thank you. We're excited. We've booked the club for our wedding. It will be the talk of the town. I'll make sure your invite includes a plus-one. Will you be bringing Shelly, or is this your new love?"

"I won't be bringing anyone to anything you and your boy, Larry, are hosting. I do wish the two of you the best of luck, though. You're going to need it."

"Where is Shelly? The two of you used to be everywhere together, but she hasn't been around in a while."

As curious as Ivy was to hear what this Brittany character knew that she didn't, Desmond's discomfort was her cue to leave.

"I'm going to the ladies' room," she informed him before grabbing her clutch and standing.

"Nice meeting you, Ivy," Brittany purred, with saccharin sincerity.

"Enjoy your evening," Ivy politely responded, glad to put distance between the unwelcomed Messy Molly and the whole unpleasant encounter.

"You ready?"

Ivy, deep in thought, hadn't noticed Desmond return from the valet stand. He placed a gentle hand on her arm and led them outside. The night was chilly, but his light touch sent heat waves through the chinchilla that scorched her skin. They stepped up to a fancy car even more beautiful than the one she'd arrived in, quite a feat since the car had been like something out of a fairy tale. He waved away the valet and opened her door. She slid into toasty seats that felt like butter and inhaled a slightly musky scent she couldn't name. Desmond entered on the driver's side and soon they were floating toward home. She leaned against the headrest and sighed.

"Did you have a good time?"

"Best night of my life."

She noted Desmond's brief satisfied grin and felt a pang of self-reproach. That spot should have belonged to Gerald and the night they became engaged. But if she were truthful, and Ivy rarely bamboozled herself, she'd have to admit that the evening paled in comparison to the one she'd just enjoyed.

"I hope Brittany didn't put too much of a damper on it."

"I heard her comment about dating Jake's best friend. Is that how you know her?"

"Everybody knows Brittany."

"You dated her, too?"

"Hell, no! I meant that in the way of how when growing up in a small town, everyone knows everyone else. Even now with our expanding population, there's usually no more than one or two degrees that separate us."

"Jake was clearly not feeling her and didn't try and hide it."

"Back in the day, she dated Jake's best friend Cayden, the brother from another mother who's been like a member of our family since he was a teen. She pulled some shenanigans that almost ruined Cayden's life. Jake forgave her but he never forgot."

"Cayden is the guy married to Avery and expecting a child."

Desmond glanced at her. "You've met him?"

"No. Your mom mentioned him during one of our visits. She and your sisters, Maeve and Reign, were discussing a baby shower they've planned for her, I believe to be held at the club we just left.

"I got the feeling you weren't fond of her fiancé, either."

"Lawrence is a part of the Kincaid family. They've always envied us and fancy themselves our competitors. Recently, they bought a bank and are now trying to woo away our customers."

They reached Desmond's mansion. He pulled around back and into the garage. They were enveloped in a semi-darkness that felt both romantic and dangerous. She opened her door.

"Let me get that."

Desmond walked around and helped her out of the car. At the touch of his hand, desire shot through her like a bolt of lightning. It was raw and unexpected and had her thinking thoughts that were inappropriate where bosses were concerned.

Just a little longer, she encouraged herself. *Another minute or two and you'll be away from this human mass of manly molten lava and back within the safe confines of your room.*

They entered the foyer and were greeted by the strong scent of roses. Instead of going up the stairs he walked over to the vase.

"Those flowers are stunning," Ivy offered, while mentally willing him to take his fine ass to bed before she lost all semblance of control, turned into a feral feline and jumped his bones.

"It's a shop my family has patronized for years. One of the best in the country."

He turned squarely toward her. His eyes dropped to her lips before meeting her gaze. "I had a lovely time tonight, Ivy."

"Me, too."

"Thank you for joining me."

"You're welcome."

"Well, um, good night."

"Good night."

He leaned over and placed a gentle kiss on her forehead, another on her cheek. In a boldness completely unlike her, Ivy tilted her head and countered with a tender kiss on his lips. She might as well have touched them with a stick of dynamite because the next thing she knew his arm encircled her waist, she reached for his neck and the kiss went from soft to scorching. She opened her mouth. His tongue slid inside as though it'd always belonged there, hers swirled around his as though welcoming him home. The kiss deepened. His hand dropped to her ass and cupped it gently. She leaned into his tall, toned frame. His hardening desire pressed against her. She moaned. The kiss deepened. Whether it lasted minutes or hours, she wasn't sure. She only knew she didn't want it to end. Instead, Desmond did the honors.

With a moan he pulled back, her name came out in a whisper. "Ivy." He placed his forehead against hers as they both worked to regain their breath.

"If we don't stop now, I might lose all control."

Ivy already had. Later, she'd reason that was the moment she lost her mind, too. That's the only explanation for why instead of backing away as the prudent Ivy would have and should have done, she pressed her hardened nipples against his chest and reached for his belt.

"Don't stop."

This response was completely out of character. She thought only of being swept away on a wave of pleasure, forgetting about Gerald's death and Bonnie's threats and her mother's health problems and out of control spending. Ivy's desire for Desmond was so overwhelming she hardly recognized that the breathless voice speaking was her own. The only thing she could comprehend was Desmond's large hands squeezing, then cupping her ass as he effortlessly lifted her into his arms and walked them through her living space, down the hall, past the nursery and into Ivy's bedroom.

He sat her gently on the bed, then caressed her face. "You're beautiful."

"Because of you. The stylists…"

He shushed her with a finger to her lips. "Not that. You. Naturally."

Without breaking eye contact, he reached for one of her designer-clad feet and slipped off a shoe. He placed a thumb in the arch of her foot and massaged it in gentle circles. Ivy couldn't understand how his touching her feet could make her moisten but her feminine folds began dripping dew.

He removed the other shoe, then pulled her up and turned her around. "Are you sure?"

In answer, Ivy reached up in an attempt to unzip her own dress.

Desmond chuckled softly, sexily, kissing each spot revealed as the zipper slid down. He eased the silky material off her shoulders, caressing her from behind. The solid evidence of his arousal pulsed against her. She swallowed. It felt massive. Could she handle him? Could she in all honesty handle any of this?

She didn't know, but she was about to find out.

"Don't stop."

This response was completely out of character. She thought only of being swept away on a wave of pleasure, forgetting about Gerald's death and Bonnie's threats and her mother's health problems and out of control spending. Ivy's desire for Desmond was so overwhelming she hardly recognized that the breathless voice speaking was her own. The only thing she could comprehend was Desmond's large hands squeezing, then cupping her ass as he effortlessly lifted her into his arms and walked them through her living space, down the hall, past the nursery and into Ivy's bedroom.

He sat her gently on the bed, then caressed her face. "You're beautiful."

"Because of you. The stylists…"

He shushed her with a finger to her lips. "Not that. You. Naturally."

Without breaking eye contact, he reached for one of her designer-clad feet and slipped off a shoe. He placed a thumb in the arch of her foot and massaged it in gentle circles. Ivy couldn't understand how his touching her feet could make her moisten but her feminine folds began dripping dew.

He removed the other shoe, then pulled her up and turned her around. "Are you sure?"

In answer, Ivy reached up in an attempt to unzip her own dress.

Desmond chuckled softly, sexily, kissing each spot revealed as the zipper slid down. He eased the silky material off her shoulders, caressing her from behind. The solid evidence of his arousal pulsed against her. She swallowed. It felt massive. Could she handle him? Could she in all honesty handle any of this?

She didn't know, but she was about to find out.

and unexpected. He held her nub in his mouth as she exploded, sucked her as though ambrosia poured from her lips. It took a while for her to realize the mewling sound in the room was her. Tears formed as her body hummed from the aftermath. She opened her eyes to see Desmond staring down at her, unbuckling his belt and letting his tuxedo slacks fall. He wore black boxers that did little to hide his enormous erection.

He was beautiful. He was a god.

Once naked, he reached for his slacks and pulled out a foil packet. Then he guided her farther onto the bed and slid in beside her. The lovemaking continued without another word. He removed her lingerie. His tongue was everywhere—breasts, stomach, arms, face. She tried to give as good as she got but she was no match for his talent. Still, she boldly wrapped her fingers around his massive girth, ran her nail along the mushroom ridge and inwardly smiled as he gasped at the pressure. Then he was on top of her. Their bodies touching. Nothing between them but a promise of a heavenly night to come. With their lips locked, he slid his fingers up and down the folds of her heat, making her even wetter than before. With infinite patience, he guided himself inside her, allowing time for her body to adjust. Ivy ignored the pain for the pleasure she knew awaited. She swirled her hips upward to meet him, to encourage his descent into her waiting walls. He would not be hurried. He pressed himself halfway in, pulled out to the tip, then in again. This seemed to go on forever until she took in his full length and they set up a lazy rhythm that Ivy knew she could enjoy for an entire lifetime. She rubbed her hands along his strong back, pushed her pebbled nipples against his hard chest, tried to stay present in the moment. Tried to remember that this was not a dream.

Desmond was a skilled and considerate lover. He

smoothly led their erotic dance, changing positions seamlessly, making her come again and again. Just when she thought she'd lose her mind from his prowess, the thrusting increased. With a low moan, Desmond went over the edge and joined Ivy in a trip to the stars.

He finished and collapsed on top of her. He was heavy but instead of discomfort, Ivy felt safe. She could feel his rapid heartbeat and knew it matched her own. A light sheen of sweat caused his body to glisten. He was almost too gorgeous to be real. She wrapped her arms around him and squeezed as tightly as possible.

"Thank you," she whispered in his ear.

He kissed her temple. "You're welcome."

Slowly, silence descended and with it, reality. Once the glow of lovemaking receded, Ivy was faced with a question.

What in the world have I done?

Fourteen

The next morning, Desmond arrived at the office with a spring in his step. Ivy's intense lovemaking had not only surprised him but revived him. For the past several months, work had consumed him. Dalliances with the opposite sex had been rare. Until that powerful orgasm, he hadn't realized how much he'd missed having regular good loving as a part of his life. Was totally floored by how much he'd enjoyed it with Ivy. He never would have guessed beneath those casual clothes and conservative nature was a tigress waiting to be unleashed. He hoped she had no regrets about what happened last night. Because already he was thinking of and hoping for a next time.

He checked his watch, then reached for his cell phone. It was early but he went ahead and sent a text. Good morning.

For several long moments, there was no answer. When it came the response was short and curt. Morning.

Desmond reached for his mug of coffee and leaned back in his chair. What did that one-word response mean? Was she happy, embarrassed, wallowing in morning-after guilt? Never one to shy away from a potential problem or challenge, he reached again for his phone. You okay?

This time the response was almost immediate.

Can we talk later? Tending to Desiree.

Okay, beautiful. Have a wonderful day.

A minute passed. Five. Ten. No answer. Desmond willed himself to focus on work but his mind had other plans. As he scrolled through his emails and checked text messages, he continued to replay last evening. How amazing Ivy looked as she stepped into the Point du Sable Country Club, her transformation nearly taking his breath away. How her quiet nature fit his extroverted one, and how while clearly not a part of the upper echelon crowd, she held her own in the environment, even against barracudas like Brittany Smith.

But it's what happened after the concert that was seared in his mind. Her body fit his perfectly and, man, how right her plump ass felt in his palms. Making love to her on a regular basis would be incredible. Of that, he had no doubt. From the way she responded to his oral talents, she'd clearly not been thoroughly loved. She wasn't worldly like Penelope and women like her. There was something akin to innocence that was not only refreshing but attractive. A naivete that made him want to protect her and be the only one invited into her bed. He wanted to be solely responsible for lighting her body on fire. After last night, the marriage of convenience idea was even more attractive. But was it fair to ask this of someone like Ivy? A woman still suffering from losing her fiancé, and one clearly not overly experienced in love? With the sound of Ivy's obvious pleasure still ringing, Desmond found himself second-guessing the wisdom of making such a drastic move. His parents had true love and a thriving marriage, the kind of relationship he eventually wanted. Someday, a moment way off in the future. Not now. Not with everything he had going on. Not with Shelly's deception so fresh and being a father so new. For him, he could still handle the arrangement as the business transaction it was. But could Ivy? He wasn't so sure.

He'd put those thoughts aside and was leading a Zoom meeting with a group of Asian banking officials ready to make E-Squared Crypto a part of their currency when the office intercom came alive.

"Excuse me for one moment, gentlemen." He muted his mic on the computer, then punched the button. "I thought I asked not to be disturbed?" His exasperation was apparent.

"I'm sorry, Desmond. It's Ernest Duvall. He said the matter was urgent and—"

"Fine, put him through."

Desmond unmuted his computer mic. "Gentlemen, can you give me five minutes?"

After a round of affirmative answers, he again muted the mic and turned off the conference call video. A picture of the company logo came up on the screen as Ernest's voice came over the speaker.

"I understand you're in the middle of a meeting, Desmond. Sorry to interrupt."

"You're only following my instructions. What do you have for me?"

"We found her."

Desmond didn't need a name to know *her* identity. For his top PI to interrupt what he was sure Janice told him was a very important meeting, it could only mean one thing. They'd found Shelly.

"Where?"

"Fiji."

"Damn. Long way from Chicago."

"Indeed. Seven thousand, two hundred and fifty-eight miles to be exact, on a direct flight."

"Is she alone?"

"Negative. An older European gentlemen has been seen going in and out of the house."

That didn't surprise Desmond. One thing about Shelly, wherever she was, she was never without a man for long. It was probably how she got to the island.

"Good work, Ernie. I appreciate it."

"What next, Mr. Eddington?"

"Give me the day to think about it. And have your passport ready. You might be flying over there within the week."

Desmond ended the call, then sent a text to Chef John and another to Ivy. Then he rang Janice.

"Call the mayor's office and reschedule my meeting for this evening. Offer my apologies but tell them something came up that requires my immediate attention."

"Is everything okay?" Janice asked.

"That's what I'm working on finding out."

The day flew by. Once back home, he changed out of his suit and went to the dining room. It was empty. He continued on to the kitchen where John was busy stirring something that smelled incredible in a stainless steel pot.

"Hey, John."

"Good evening, sir."

"Have you seen Ivy?"

"I believe she's downstairs, sir, caring for the baby. Earlier she came and requested a puree of organic apples. She thinks the child may be teething. Would you like to have dinner served down there?"

"That'll be fine, John. Thanks."

Desmond went downstairs. Ivy was in the living room, holding Desiree. She immediately put a finger to her lips. He nodded and quietly entered. She placed the child on her shoulder, rocking her gently. After she'd placed Desiree in her crib, she returned to where Desmond waited.

"Sorry about not meeting you at seven as requested. The baby's been fussy all day."

"No worries. John will be setting up a dinner service there." He nodded toward a bistro table by the window that looked out on a fountain.

"Okay." They sat down over there.

"John tells me Desiree doesn't feel well, that she's teething?"

"That seems most likely. Normally, that doesn't start until the fourth or fifth month, but research tells me that some begin as early as three months, as Desiree is now.

"I assume you're here to talk about last night."

"Being with you was amazing but actually, no, that wasn't the reason for my text. I learned some news today and wanted to discuss it with you."

Ivy didn't respond, simply looked at him with those wide bright eyes that last night almost hypnotized him.

"We've found Shelly."

"Oh." Said with a face devoid of expression. "Where?"

"The Fiji Islands."

"Wow, you located her way over there?"

"It took some doing but, yes, my guys found her."

"And?"

"I don't know, which is why I wanted to speak with you, get the perspective of a levelheaded female on what you think is the best action to take."

"You're just wanting her to sign the NDA, correct?"

"That and grant us sole custody."

"Ah." She drew out the word in understanding. "That could prove tricky."

"Why do you say that? For all intents and purposes, Desiree was abandoned."

"It's one thing to leave one's child with the father where you're assured she'll be cared for. I'd imagine signing away one's rights legally is another one altogether."

"How would you approach her?"

They paused as John arrived with chunks of freshly baked bread and bowls of an Indian-inspired chickpea soup, the spicy scents of curry and coconut tickling both their noses and making Desmond's mouth water.

Ivy tasted the soup, closed her eyes and moaned. "Oh, my god. That's incredible."

Her face was thoughtful as she enjoyed another spoonful, then wiped her mouth with a napkin.

"I'd treat each matter separately. Get the signed NDA and broach the subject of permanent custody somewhere down the line."

Desmond nodded slowly. He broke off a piece of bread, dipped it into the soup and ate it. "I don't often eat Indian dishes but John outdid himself with one."

"I love ethnic dishes—Indian, Mexican, African, Chinese. I think I just love delicious food, no matter the culture."

They continued chatting while eating. Desmond purposely avoided what happened last night. Instead, he chose topics ranging from favorite foods to Desiree's irritability, then back around to Fiji and how best to approach his child's mother about the NDA without her getting upset. Having known each other since childhood, Desmond wouldn't be surprised if Shelly found such a request offensive and knew how unreasonable she could be when on the defense.

John returned with an entrée of chepala vepudu, hearty fish steaks marinated in a garam masala paste, deep-fried and served on a bed of rice. Ivy took a couple bites, then abruptly set down her fork.

"You don't like it?"

She shook her head. "The food is delicious. I just thought of something." She looked up at him, her gaze bereft of its usual brightness. "You could act on what I first suggested and ask Shelly to marry you. That would alleviate any potential concern she'd have about signing the NDA and solve the concern of Desiree altogether."

"Yes," Desmond responded after a pause. "I could do that."

"We're discussing options." She shrugged. "That is one."

Desiree announced she'd awakened with a healthy howl. Ivy went in to tend to her. Desmond retired to his suite, bothered by Ivy's suggestion. It was one that made sense, one that would indeed solve all the potential PR problems that news of his sudden parentage could cause and one he was sure would please Shelly immensely. So why did it feel better when imagining a marriage of convenience with the nanny than it did when considering a more genuine commitment with the mother of his child?

Fifteen

Ivy finished a temperamental Desiree's bath and dressed her in a designer onesie that while cute was hardly worth the hefty price tag she'd snipped off last week before washing it and putting it away. For the rest of last night and all day today, she'd been cranky with an elevated fever that had Ivy concerned. After giving her a cooling bath and watching Desiree down nearly four ounces of formula, her charge was fast asleep. Ivy took time to tidy up before sitting down for what she hoped would be a couple of hours of quiet time. She needed to think, and possibly plan for a life outside Eddington Estate. If Desmond followed her advice regarding Shelly, she could soon be out of a job. After last night, Ivy wasn't sure she should continue watching Desiree. There was no way she could stay on if he and Shelly got married. As it was, the two needed to have a serious conversation. As much as she'd loved everything about her fairy-tale evening, that's just what it was. A fantasy. Not reality. A real-life dream that, as much as she wanted it, couldn't happen again. Nor could a marriage of convenience. There was no way she could fake what was happening inside her, the inconvenience of falling in love.

Dammit!

She should have listened to her mother and stayed in her place. Sought out companionship with a man of similar background. It was ridiculous to have feelings for a man like Desmond who was totally out of her reach. Her head knew this. Her heart hadn't listened. And her body, well, it was still on fire. Just the thought of his touch could harden her nipples and make her wet. One look, and Ivy was sure Shelly would be able to detect her feelings about Desmond. Women had a special radar for things like that. It took men a bit longer to catch on in love matters. Still, Ivy was finding it harder to hide her feelings from Desmond. Perhaps Shelly returning and her leaving would be best for them all.

Ivy blew out a breath and reached for her planner, the one she preferred to the app on her tablet. Tapping a pen against the pages, her mind drifted from thoughts of her girl's school to finding a different type of employment, one where she wouldn't become so emotionally invested, fall in love with her employer or grow accustomed to a lifestyle that would never fully be hers. She'd worked hard to retain her ordinariness in the midst of such opulence. But one thing Ivy had quickly grown fond of was the exceptional food served in Desmond's home. John reminded her of a favorite uncle. Of all the staff and family, the chef was the one she felt most comfortable around and on the two or three days a week he came over to prepare meals for their household, they'd struck up a great friendship. He'd even offered to teach her to cook, something her mother had never considered a high priority and her schooling didn't teach. Until then, she was content to do as she did now, head up to the subzero stainless stocked full of fabulous food and find something she could munch on while working. After deciding on a trio of salads—salmon, quinoa and kale—she grabbed a bag of sweet potato chips and a bottle of Kona Nigari and headed back downstairs. She would have been fine with Perrier, Fiji or good old Great Value, and had initially refused to drink any after a quick Google search revealed it sold for four hundred dollars a bottle, but the designer water was the only kind Desmond stocked and she had to admit the taste was notably different and delicious. That was one of many surprises Ivy had encountered in her first month as nanny. Almost everything about the wealthy lifestyle was different, even the food.

She'd just taken a few bites and fired up her tablet when her cell phone rang. *Unless it's Mama or Desmond, I'm not answering.*

It was Lynn. "Or you." She tapped the phone icon and put the call on speaker.

"Hey, Lynn."

"Good afternoon, Ivy."

"Please excuse my chewing in your ear. I just put the baby down and fixed a plate."

"No worries. This won't take long. I just realized we hadn't chatted for a few weeks. I'm just checking in. How's life as Desiree's nanny? Everything still going okay?"

Desmond's glistening, naked body flashed before her. "Everything's fine."

"Look, after what happened during our last phone call, I know you're hesitant about providing details."

"Yes, very." That and the fact that I've been screwed by my boss to within an inch of my life and have a marriage of convenience proposal on the table.

"But it's important that I have a general idea of how things are going to be able to update your files. We'll focus on the child, not the father. Does that work better for you?"

"Desiree is a wonderful baby, she really is. She's ahead of the curve when it comes to her learning and is generally well-behaved. She's in the early stages of teething, though, and has been cranky for the past couple of days."

"Wow, she's early. How old is she?"

"Thirteen weeks."

"I think Isaac Jr. began at four months so that sounds about right."

They spoke a bit more about a child's stages of development, when Lynn steered the convo in another direction.

"On a scale of one to ten, how would you rate the interaction with…your employer?"

Twenty! Ivy took a sip of water and forced a nonchalance in her voice that she was far from feeling.

"A solid seven, maybe eight." And the Academy Award goes to…!

"Wow, that's great!"

Ivy speculated that Lynn wanted to know more but she wasn't going to say anything that would invalidate the NDA. With all of the AI electronics wired throughout the house, she knew that even the walls had ears.

"Yes. It's been a big adjustment for everyone but I'm growing more confident in my skills and the regimen I've created for Desiree, which makes me more comfortable, too."

"That's really great to hear, Ivy. I knew you'd be a perfect fit."

Ivy's phone beeped. "Lynn, it's Desmond on the other line. Can I call you back?"

"No need. I'll update your files and we'll talk at the six-month mark of your employment."

"Sounds good. Thanks, Lynn." Pouring water from the bottle into a glass, she tapped the screen.

"Hi, Desmond."

"Hey, Ivy. Just checking on Desi. How's she doing?"

"You know, I think that's the first time you've called to ask about her. Very good, Dad!"

They shared a laugh.

"She was still cranky this morning but after a bath and a bottle she fell fast asleep."

"That's good to hear."

"Desmond, we need to—"

"I talked to Shelly."

"You did?"

"Yes. It's the other reason for my call. I took your advice and spoke of the NDA with no mention of my desire for sole custody."

"And?"

"The request didn't go over well. It might take me flying over for an in-person conversation to convince her. If so, I'll more than likely be gone for about a week."

The thought of going that long without seeing Desmond caused a pang in Ivy's heart.

"Do you think you can keep the household running without me?"

"With Chauncey, Bernice, John and your mom, I'm sure I can handle anything."

"You're probably right about that. I feel better already."

"I'm glad."

"I wanted to let you know as soon as possible, and apologize for interrupting. You were about to say something?"

"Yes, about last night."

"I hope you don't feel badly about that. I enjoyed every moment of the evening. You were incredible from beginning to end."

"I...liked it, too. Perhaps too much. I honestly don't know what got into me but I do know that it can never happen again."

"Are you sure that's what you want?"

"It's what has to happen."

"I can't lie and say that I'm not disappointed but, of course, I'll honor your choice. I do hope, however, that the proposal we discussed isn't off the table. Our getting married, temporarily, and my funding your school."

"I don't know, Desmond..."

"Hey, let's do this. Let's take this week and think about it, what do you say? We'll be apart with enough physical and mental space between us to think clearly."

"Or Shelly could prove to be the answer you need."

"I doubt that. In the meantime, do you have anything written up concerning the girl's school?"

"I have the complete business plan."

"Great. Do me a favor and email it over. It'll give me something to read on the plane."

For the next couple days, Ivy didn't see much of Desmond, though he did send a text that he'd booked a flight to Fiji for the following week. Desiree continued to be cranky, causing Ivy to lose even more of her much-needed sleep and put grant writing and school planning on hold. One good thing, however, was the warmer weather that spring had welcomed. Once the baby was better, Ivy planned to walk instead of drive to the main house for Desiree's visits with Mona. A wail splitting the silence told Ivy today was definitely not that day.

"I'm coming, little one," she said, quickly pulling the top of a two-piece yoga outfit over her head and heading to the nursery. "I need to order that amber necklace," she mumbled, remembering the article she'd read in a holistic magazine about the crystal's ability to sooth minor pains.

She reached the crib and immediately noticed Desiree's reddish color. Felt her skin and quickly pulled back her hand. She didn't need a thermometer to know the child's fever had raised through the night. A minute later, the infrared thermometer confirmed her assumption. Desiree's temperature was 103 degrees.

After hurrying back into her bedroom and retrieving the phone, she called Mona. "Hi, Mona. It's Ivy, calling about Desiree. Her temperature has spiked. I'm very concerned that she needs to be seen by a doctor. What should I do?"

"Sit tight. I'll have my personal physician Dr. Harrison come right over."

Less than thirty minutes later, there was a knock on Ivy's door. A nice-looking man wearing khakis and carrying a black leather bag stood at the door.

"Dr. Harrison?" He nodded. "Please, come in."

"Where is the little one?"

"Back here. Mona isn't with you?"

"She was attending a breakfast meeting in Chicago but is on her way."

The doctor performed a thorough examination. Mona arrived halfway through. When finished, he pulled off his stethoscope and placed it and other items he'd used back in the black bag.

"Well, Gene?" Mona's anxiety was palpable. Ivy, too, was on edge.

"I could bring over a portable X-ray machine, but I did take blood and other samples to send to the lab. Considering her fever, though, Mona, I wouldn't wait for those results. I understand your need for discretion, but she needs to be in a hospital to receive the best care."

"Will they admit her without the birth mom being present?"

"They will after I make a few calls."

Ivy called Desmond and provided an update. His genuine concern was touching and made her even more determined to make sure Desiree received the best care. After getting the green light from Dr. Harrison, she and Mona rode in her humble Kia to PDS Medical and were directed to the private entrance of a special wing used by high-profile citizens not wanting anyone to know about their hospital stay. They were greeted by a nurse named Tami, who Mona informed was Cayden's mom, and ushered into a room that looked more like one you'd see in an upscale home instead of a hospital. The walls were a soothing shade of blue with not a fluorescent light in sight. It was decided that Desmond and the rest of the fam would stay in touch remotely. Too many Eddingtons around might draw attention, even with the privacy protocol. Dr. Harrison arrived and met with the specialists, then returned to the room.

"She needs to stay here for a few days," he informed them. "They've managed to reduce the fever but have ordered more extensive blood-work analysis."

"Are you in touch with the mother?" he asked Mona.

"She's being contacted," Mona replied.

"If for any reason we're not able to treat her properly and she needs to see a specialist in another location, it will be hard to get around protocol. Either a parent or legal guardian will have to approve whatever treatment is recommended."

Mona gave a curt nod but took on a look that hinted to Ivy of where Desmond got some of his backbone. She had no doubt that papers or no papers, legal or not, Desiree would get the best treatment that money could buy...by any means necessary.

Sixteen

For Desmond, fear was a rarely felt emotion. In this moment, however, as he waited for Shelly to answer his call, he felt the first true bonds of fatherhood. Until now, he'd viewed Desiree as a mistake at worst and an inconvenient blessing at best. In this moment, she was his daughter, one he did not want to lose.

"Hello?"

"Shelly, it's Desmond."

"I know who it is."

"Sure. Right. I'm glad you picked up."

"Why? So you can threaten me into buying my silence and signing away my parental rights?"

"You dropped off Desiree like an Amazon package. I didn't take her away."

"You know what? I don't need this…"

Desmond gritted his teeth to stop the sarcastic response on the tip of his tongue. Desiree's health issue had changed his plans and caused an alteration of Ivy's soft-pedal suggestion. Last night, he'd been forced to request his name on his daughter's birth certificate and ask for primary custody because, he reasoned, he was the sole parent in the United States.

"I'm sorry, Shelly. Please, don't hang up."

"I told you I'd sign the NDA but only with modifications. To not be able to tell anyone I have a child is not a decision to be made lightly, or fast. As for custody, again, I need time to think about it."

"We don't have time." Desmond ran an exasperated hand over his soft tight coils and wished he could blink and be in Fiji. "Desiree's...not feeling well."

"Babies get sick, Des, and then they get better. A baby aspirin or two and I'm sure she'll be fine."

"She's in the hospital." He closed his eyes and waited for the fallout.

"Why didn't you tell me that earlier?"

"We were hoping our private physician and the specialists he recommended would be able to ascertain what was producing the fever and rectify it."

"How long has she had a fever?"

"A few days."

"A few days?" Shelly shrilled, her voice getting louder by the second. "I'm coming home."

"Not until we come to an understanding of how we'll share this information."

"I don't give a damn about your family's business, which I'm sure is all you care about."

"That's not true. I care about Desiree. A scandal would hurt her as much as me."

"What a load of crap. She's only a baby."

"Babies grow up and digital news lives forever. But it's

not just that. Because this couldn't be treated at home and she had to be admitted, there could be legal ramifications."

"Why?"

"Because I'm not listed as her legal guardian."

"Or her father."

"Exactly. Getting the signed paperwork overnighted to me will alleviate these problems."

"And me in the process. Desiree getting sick is awfully convenient, don't you think?"

"Do you think I'm lying? Come on, Shelly. I don't want to fight. I want to take care of Desiree. She's my primary concern."

"I'll think about it."

"Have you heard a word I've said? We don't have that kind of time." Silence. "Shelly?" Desmond looked down and saw a blank screen. Shelly had ended the call.

Late that night, after being discreetly allowed into the hospital's private wing to see his daughter, Desmond arrived home to find Ivy waiting.

"Any change?" she asked, nervously chewing her bottom lip.

Even with his mind solely on Desiree, the memory of how sweet that lip tasted flashed in his head.

"She's still stable, but they're stumped on what's causing the fever. They're also concerned with a rare enzyme found in her blood. If she's not better by this time tomorrow, Dr. Harrison suggests she be transferred to Trinity Children's Hospital in Manhattan."

"New York?"

Desmond nodded. "When it comes to pediatrics, he says they're the best."

Once again, Desmond's sleep was fitful but at the office he managed to get some work done. With Ivy and his mother keeping watch at the hospital, and intermittent visits from his sisters, Maeve and Reign, he felt less guilty about working. Mona adored her first grandchild, and he had no doubt that Ivy loved the little girl as much as he did. When Janice delivered his mail, he quickly rummaged through it, hoping an express mail from Fiji would have somehow arrived. There was nothing and worse, Shelly had stopped talking. His calls went straight to voice mail, increasing his frustration along with his angst. He left work early and headed straight for PDS Medical. He was driving his Bentley and would be more conspicuous. He didn't care. Nothing mattered right now but the health of his daughter. The longer it took for them to properly diagnose her, the deeper his concern. By the time he'd pulled around to the underground garage that led to one of the wing's private entrances, he was actually nervous. He hadn't expected her, hadn't known he wanted to be a father. Now he couldn't imagine life without Desiree in it, or what he'd do if something happened to his baby girl.

He was the lone passenger in the elevator to the wing's lobby. Once there, he went directly to the corner suite where Desiree was being treated. He entered quietly. Ivy and Tami, one of only two nurses approved for the room, were sitting at the table, their heads together. As soon as they saw him, both Tami and Ivy got up and walked over, their faces tight with what looked like apprehension. He glanced over at Desiree who seemed to be sleeping peacefully.

Tami reached him first. "Desmond, I'm so glad you're here."

"What's wrong?"

"We have a bit of a problem."

Desmond's stomach clenched. "What is it?"

"Michelle is here, or she was, looking for Desiree."

His outer calm belied a slow burning anger that he knew if not contained, would explode.

Ivy placed a comforting hand on his arm. "Has she called you?"

"No, but that explains why she's been unavailable for twenty-four hours. Where is she?"

"I don't know. She appeared at the front desk, demanding to see Desiree. As fate would have it, I was at the nurse's station, heard the commotion and took her into my office. Told her to sit tight until I got her visit approved. Then I came here, talked to Ivy and was just about to call when you walked in the door. What should I do?"

Desmond ran a hand over his face. "Damn."

"I don't think she's going away," Ivy offered. "I wouldn't, if it were my child."

Tami nodded in agreement. "Nor would I."

"Is there a way you can bring her here without others seeing?"

Again, Tami nodded, this time with a tight smile.

"Then go get her."

Ivy's questions began as soon as the door was closed. Both the wing and the room were ultra-private. Still, Ivy whispered, "How did she know about Desiree's illness?"

"I told her. I thought it would help expedite her signing the papers, so that I would have legal authority to have Desiree transferred."

He strode to the window, his anger again mounting. "That's what I get for being considerate. I could have had forged papers drawn up with you as her mother and no one would have been the wiser."

"That wouldn't have been right, or fair to Shelly."

"Maybe not, but it's what I should have done."

He returned to the bed, placed his hand on Desiree's

forehead. "She feels cooler," he marveled. "Some of her color has returned."

"Dr. Harrison has been a near-constant presence, staying on top of the specialists, monitoring their results."

"He and my dad go back to high school. He's known all of us since before we were born."

The two were quiet for several moments, standing next to each other, looking down at the baby. Without thinking, Desmond placed an arm around Ivy's shoulder and gave it a squeeze.

She leaned her head on his arm and rubbed her hand across his back. "Try to stay calm when you see Desiree's mother. Try and believe that everything will be fine."

The door opened. Both Desmond and Ivy turned as Tami entered the room, followed by a woman who looked and smelled like wealth. She tossed a thick head of black hair over her shoulder, strode to the bed without speaking in five-inch heels.

"Hello, Shelly," Desmond said, his voice low and controlled.

"Desmond," Shelly replied without looking up.

Her eyes were on Desiree. She hesitantly touched the babe's forehead and cheek, awkwardly patted the blanket covering her. Desmond felt Ivy begin to move away from him. He lightly gripped her arm to stop her. That's when Shelly looked up. She looked at his hand on her arm, then from Desmond to Ivy.

"Who are you?"

"She's Desiree's nanny, Shelly. Her name is Ivy. She's the one who's been taking excellent care of our child."

Seventeen

Ivy's first thought? She's a very pretty woman, striking actually. Her second, there would be no marriage of mutual convenience. How could she compete with Shelly, or any woman as beautiful as her? It was crazy to have thought such a thing was even remotely possible, even under circumstances like the one Desmond was in. All of this went through her head in the seconds it took to extend her hand and attempt a smile.

"Nice to meet you," she said.

Shelly's feeble handshake came with a judgmental once-over. "Thanks for helping with my daughter but I'm here now. You can go back to the house—" she waved her hand dismissively "—and do whatever you do there."

"This is her work," Desmond responded, in a commanding tone that brooked no argument and before Ivy could take a step. "She's spent more time with Desiree than anyone else," he added in a gentler tone.

"Even so, I'm the mom. She's the help. I don't want her here."

"Too bad. She's under my employ. You're the trespasser. I'm in charge of who stays or goes."

So much for being calm, Ivy thought, feeling uneasy. The look Desmond gave Shelly suggested she might be the one making an exit. Shelly must have gotten the nonverbal message. She wisely chose to be quiet. Little did she know, for as much as Ivy was concerned about Desiree, she wanted to leave the room more than Shelly wanted her to go. The situation was awkward to say the least, one that with each silence-coated second grew more uncomfortable.

Dr. Harrison entered the room. He looked at Shelly, then at Desmond.

"It's okay for her to be here. What have you learned?"

The doctor pulled off his glasses and wiped them with a handkerchief from his pocket. "The team agrees she'd be better where the staff specializes in pediatrics."

"Trinity Children's Hospital."

"Exactly, right. I've already talked to the hospital president and explained the situation. He's a brother," Dr. Harrison added, referring to the powerful Society.

Desmond visibly relaxed.

"Being in New York, they're used to dealing with high-profile patients. They've handled celebrity pregnancies and childbirth and other sensitive medical issues that needed to be kept out of the public eye. I gave him your number. He'll be calling directly. The hospital's private plane is fueled and ready." He looked around the room. "Whoever is flying to New York with the baby needs to be ready within the hour."

Desmond held out his hand. "Thanks, doc. I owe you one."

"I'll take it in the form of floor seats for the next Bulls game."

"You got it."

The two men exchanged a fraternity handshake before the doctor bid goodbye to the women and left. Ivy turned to follow him out.

Desmond called after her. "Ivy, wait. Where are you going?"

"Home to grab the baby bible where Desiree's records are stored. I didn't think to bring it here but it might help when you talk to the doctors in New York."

She left without giving Desmond time to answer. She needed fresh air, and space away from Shelly.

Once home and in the sanctity of her suite, Ivy plopped into a chair. The reality of the situation came crashing down around her. The status of nanny had never been clearer. Shelly's instant dislike had been apparent. Ivy could only imagine how it must have looked when Shelly walked in there. Her and Desmond practically hugged up by Shelly's daughter's bed. There was no need to ponder long on this scenario's obvious conclusion. Ivy's days as Desiree's nanny were numbered. It was time to find a job.

She jumped up, walked into the nursery and retrieved the baby bible, which she placed into a diaper bag along with some of Desiree's things. Tears threatened as she imagined her life without Desiree in it, with no reason to interact with the baby's dad. The downstairs door opened. Ivy started at the unexpected noise.

"Ivy!"

"In here, Desmond." She pulled herself together and had just zipped up the diaper bag when Desmond strode into the room.

"Pack a bag for yourself as well. You're going to New York."

"Me? What about Shelly?"

"Dr. Harrison limited the number of people who could fly with his patient, and said since you're Desiree's primary caregiver, you should definitely be one of them. Shelly and Mama will fly up tomorrow."

"And she was okay with that?"

"She had to be." An impish smile flitted across Desmond's face, replacing the worried expression with a boyish charm. "Personally, I think the good doctor did me a favor. I'm familiar with the type of plane they fly and while I'm sure it's configured in a way that limits seating, there was probably room for at least one more passenger. The way he explained it made it hard for Shelly not to cooperate if she wanted what's best for the child."

"I don't know, Desmond. It was clear that she doesn't like me. I don't want to cause any trouble."

"Then don't argue with me. Trust me, I'll handle Shelly. That is if my mother doesn't get to her first. She's not forgiven her for putting her granddaughter in a box, let alone leaving said box in the hands of a stranger. When I told her about Shelly being here, Mama Bear came into full effect."

He looked at his watch. "Let me run up and pack a bag. We need to get to the airstrip ASAP."

"You're going, too?"

"Of course, I'm going. Do you think I'd let you handle this crisis alone?"

One of the staff drove Desmond and Ivy to the airstrip, where they took off less than fifteen minutes after boarding the plane. Tami was onboard along with one of the specialists. Ivy looked around. Desmond was right. There was plenty more room on the plane. It was a quiet trip that went by very quickly. Once in New York, Desiree was transferred by helicopter to Trinity Children's. A limo picked up Desmond and Ivy. Forty-five minutes later, they were ushered into a building much older than PDS Medical Center and not as plush, but from the quiet, unobtrusive way the staff went about their business, it was obviously just as efficient and discreet.

They were there for an hour. After meeting with the specialists and getting Desiree tucked into her new hospital bed, the president of the hospital called Desmond personally to assure that Desiree would receive the best of care and that rest was what he needed. With that guarantee, the two headed downstairs to a waiting town car that whisked them uptown. It had been years since Ivy had visited New York, and then most of her time had been spent with her college friend's family in Brooklyn. She remembered being caught up in the excitement of the city's constant buzz but tonight as she gazed out of the town car window, she barely saw a thing. She was concerned for Desiree, confused about Shelly's absence and trepidatious about how the night would play out.

She needn't have worried. Halfway to their destination, Desmond got a call. It was Janice, reminding him of the conference call she'd arranged per his request with the board of directors of a prestigious financial services company in Sydney, Australia. The time was set for 10:00 a.m. in Australia, which was eight o'clock in New York. Desmond was clearly frazzled. The normally meticulous businessman had forgotten all about it, his mind only on Desiree and what the doctors would find. When they reached the Park Lane Hotel across from Central Park, Desmond stole away to one of two master bedrooms to prepare for his meeting. Ivy spoke with the concierge and had dinner delivered. When she finished her pizza, Desmond was still on the call. She intended to stay awake until he finished. But she lay down and almost before her head hit the pillow fell fast asleep, and dreamed of the baby…and Desmond.

* * *

A soft tap on the door pulled Ivy from a light sleep. She blinked, temporarily confused, then was awed by the sight in her doorway. Desmond, wearing a T-shirt and shorts. Looking like the way she preferred her coffee—sweet, black and piping hot.

She sat up against the backboard and cleared her throat, feeling vulnerable in her skimpy nighty, as memories from another night when she literally showed her ass washed over her. Her cheeks warmed even as she worked to erase the memory.

"What time is it?"

"A little after seven."

"And you're already up?"

"And finished my workout. Mom called. She's on her way."

"Any word from the hospital?"

He shook his head. "Not yet. I figured once Mom got here, we'd head over together."

"Is Shelly arriving with your mother?"

"She decided not to come."

"Why not?"

Desmond shrugged. "I don't know."

Ivy felt guilty at how relieved the news made her. When Mona Eddington showed up a short time later, wearing a politically incorrect full-length sable and knee-high boots, she was indeed very much alone.

"Good morning," she announced to them jointly, looking as though she was responsible for the sun that peeked in between the blinds. Anyone seeing her wouldn't dare question the likelihood. Mona was beautiful, cultured and timelessly chic. She entered, pulling off her coat and casually tossing five figures on the couch.

"Good morning, Mama." Desmond gave his mother a hug. He looked behind her.

"Hello, Mona," Ivy said from the kitchen, with a wave.

"Hi, Ivy."

"I was just fixing a cup of coffee. Would you like one?"

"Thank you, Ivy, but no. I'm fine."

Desmond followed his mother into the living room. "What happened with Shelly?"

"She decided that it would be in her best interest to remain in the Point until you got back there, and the two of you have had a chance to…iron out your differences."

Ivy watched as Desmond's eyes narrowed. He crossed his arms. "Mom…"

"It wasn't my doing," Mona responded. "I called to suggest she and I fly out together. She said something had come up, she'd changed her mind and to keep her posted."

"Something more important than Desiree?"

"Now your focus can truly be solely on Desi. Consider it a blessing, son."

"You're right. Thanks, Mama." He heard a beep on his phone and checked the text. "Dammit."

"What?" Ivy asked.

"The statesman from the Republic of the Congo needs to set up a phone call. I forgot to call Janice and have her clear my calendar for today."

"Son, if it's urgent, Ivy and I can go to the hospital and keep you abreast of the situation. You're not just working for you now, but for your legacy. It's important to keep stacking that generational wealth."

Desmond's shoulders sagged in relief. "Are you sure?"

"Positive," Ivy said, walking in from the kitchen. "If you give me thirty minutes to shower and dress, Mona, we can be on our way."

"You can do all that in thirty minutes and still look so

pretty? Son, you might want to think about upgrading Ivy's role in your household."

For the next several days, Ivy rarely saw Desmond. He was in and out of New York. Even when there, visits to the hospital were interspersed with meetings on Wall Street. Maeve flew up one afternoon. Jake and Derrick called for updates. Mona was a constant presence. Finally, five days after they arrived, a breakthrough. Desiree was diagnosed with having a rare autoimmune disease that affected her blood cells. It was serious yet treatable. With proper medication, the specialist who set up the treatment plan, one that included alternative and holistic solutions, was cautiously optimistic that Desiree could heal from and grow out of the illness before reaching her teens.

On Friday, while Desmond finished up a meeting with the president of Trinity Children's Medical, one that included making a sizeable donation to the facility on behalf of the family's foundation, Ivy packed and prepared to fly home. She was surprised when a knock at the door of the suite revealed a smiling Mona, wearing her trademark fur.

Ivy looked at her watch. "I thought Desiree's release wasn't for another hour."

"It isn't," Mona said, breezing in without waiting for an invitation as though she owned not only the room but the hotel itself and the block it was built on. "But you don't have to worry about that."

"Why not?"

"Ivy, my family will never be able to thank you for the care and concern you've shown Desiree. You've been tireless in your effort to ensure my grandchild's well-being, starting with that baby bible, the first of its kind that I've seen. I'm impressed with your work and I don't impress easily. Someday you'll make a wonderful mother."

"Thank you," Ivy said, overcome with emotion for a

variety of reasons and afraid that if she said anything else, she'd break out into an all-out boo-hoo.

"That's not why I stopped by. I came over to inform you that you've been given the weekend off to enjoy this wonderful city."

"But, Mona—"

"No buts. It's time to focus on you for a change. Have you been here before?"

"Yes, a long time ago."

"Taken in Broadway, shopped Fifth Avenue, been given a personal tour of Harlem and all the history it contains?"

"No, and truly, it all sounds amazing. But really, I'm not adventurous like that. I'd be lucky to venture farther than a walk in Central Park, maybe, and only then if there were enough people and it was the middle of the day."

"I agree. It wouldn't be any fun to do those things alone. Which is why I've insisted that Desmond stay with you. He's been burning the candle at both ends, too. You both need a break."

Ivy thought she was speechless before. Now she felt deaf and mute. Surely, she didn't just hear what she thought she had, that Mona had set her up to spend a weekend with her firstborn.

"I'm sure Desmond has much better things to do."

"Honey, you're selling yourself way too short. A person can only value you as much as you value yourself."

Again, Ivy was in unfamiliar territory. Helen had done the best she could but her mother had never been overly generous with compliments. But Mona was right. If nothing else, Ivy knew she was an expert when it came to childcare. She'd graduated at the top of her class and was well on her way to earning her Ph.D. The past year and a half had been so tumultuous, Ivy hadn't taken the time to sit back and reflect on her achievements. She'd never been boastful, or self-centered. But it wouldn't hurt to give herself credit when and where it was due.

"What about Desiree?"

"Tami, Cayden's mother, will step in for you. She's family, and has managed to get the time off from the hospital. She'll spend the weekend with us at the Estate. It's actually perfect since next Sunday is Avery's baby shower. When not watching Desiree, we can finalize those plans."

Mona's text indicator dinged. "That's probably the driver. I told him I'd be down in five minutes fifteen minutes ago." She sent off a reply text, re-pocketed her phone and headed for the door. "Don't worry about Desiree. Relax and have fun. And remember what I told you. Don't sell yourself short. You've got a whole lot going for you, Ivy Campbell. You can give any of those women in the Point a run for all of their money."

Eighteen

Desmond had been to New York countless times. Had been wined and dined by high-end clients and at times returned the favor. But it had been years since he'd viewed the city through tourist eyes, as he now did with Ivy. It gave him a new appreciation for all the metropolis had to offer, its jewels as seen through Ivy's eyes.

After Mona left and they'd eaten at the restaurant of a celebrity chef, they were whisked to a helipad and given a helicopter tour of the city. They flew around the Statue of Liberty, close enough to see the excruciatingly intricate details of its copper design. They flew over all of the popular landmarks—Empire State, the Chrysler Building, Wall Street, Central Park, Yankee Stadium, Coney Island—with colorful commentary provided by their pilot, a native New Yorker. That evening, they dined aboard a yacht that circled the island, eating steak and lobster prepared by another world-renowned chef. The next day, they donned comfy footwear and walked the streets of Harlem, took subways to Brooklyn, Queens and the Bronx, and ate classics like warm pretzels slathered with mustard, gyros, pitas and Coney dogs "with everything" from street carts parked on every other corner. While Ivy basked in a spa and the company of a personal shopper, Desmond returned to the hotel and worked out in the gym. They came back together in time to see the venerable *The Lion King* on Broadway, then traipsed through Times Square with the rest of the tourists. There were as many people hanging out at midnight as there had been at noon. Ivy couldn't believe it. Desmond basked in her childlike joy.

Last night, they'd returned to their respective private suites. They hadn't made love. Tonight, Desmond hoped that would change. His opening came shortly after they'd returned to the hotel and were standing on the balcony, enjoying a glass of wine.

Ivy eased out of her shoes. "Today was amazing but my feet are killing me."

"It would probably help to soak them," Desmond suggested. "That and a good foot massage."

"That sounds amazing. What time is our flight tomorrow? Maybe I can sneak in an appointment before we leave."

Desmond took a step toward her. "You don't have to wait until then. I can do it."

"I don't know if that would be a good idea."

"Why not?"

"There's this funny thing that happened the last time I got close to you like that."

"What?"

"My clothes fell off."

"Ha!" Such a joke coming from Ivy was as unexpected

as it was delightful. He pulled her into his arms. "Come here."

With a kiss to her forehead, he moved behind her and pulled her against his chest so they could both gaze out on the stunning view below them. "I won't lie and say I'm not attracted to you, Ivy. But nothing will happen that you don't want."

"That's what I'm afraid of."

They stood there, quiet, Desmond's mind flickering from one thought to the next. It felt so good and right to be here with Ivy instead of Shelly taking care of his child. She felt perfect in his arms. He had no doubt she'd make a great wife and an excellent mother. But not for him. He wasn't ready yet for that lifetime commitment. On the other hand, he'd do whatever necessary to prevent Desiree's presence from becoming a scandal, including marriage. But only on paper, only temporary. If he could convince Ivy to go along with the plan, his daddy problems would be over.

She shifted away from him, still eyeing the view. "I think I will go in and take a bath. With all of that walking I did today, I'm sure my legs will thank me."

"Sure I can't help you?"

"Positive."

She turned and gave him a brief kiss on the lips. "Thank you so much for these past two days. They were incredible. I had no idea how much I needed the break."

They headed inside. "That makes two of us."

Ivy continued down the hall to her master suite. Desmond refilled his wine glass and went to his own. He stripped, showered and placed his naked body against the cool soft sheets. With only the glow of the New York night lighting his room, he casually sipped his wine and scrolled through his cell phone, checking texts, emails and social-media sites. About forty minutes later, he heard the click of a latch, then watched in subtle amazement as his door opened.

Ivy stepped in, dropped the thick white towel that covered her body and said four magical words.

"I changed my mind."

His dick, already exposed, began to harden. He opened his arms as she neared the bed. She eased into them, this time taking the lead, kissing him deeply and hungrily while she rubbed his shaft. He luxuriated in the soft feel of her freshly washed skin, the smell of desire and promise, like spring after winter, sunlight after a storm. Before he could get over the surprise of her entering his bedroom, she offered another. Soft kisses on his broad chest and taut abdomen as she continued down to his sex. He held his breath while her fingers surrounded and squeezed it, running the length of it down and up again. When she placed tentative lips around his mushroom tip, nothing could have prepared him for the jolt that shot through his body. She lightly swirled her tongue around the rimmed edge before taking him in as fully as possible, all the while stroking the base and fondling his sacs. He tried to restrain himself, but his hips wouldn't let him. They thrust up slowly, encouraging her to take in more, imitating the movement that would take on deeper meaning once inside her. To prevent himself from coming too soon, he shifted his attention to Ivy's round ass, now waving enticingly in the air, illuminated by the light coming in from outside. He squeezed her cheeks, spread them and kissed her there.

She squealed. He smiled and kissed her some more. Then it was go time.

Desmond took over. He guided her to her knees and after sliding his fingers between her already wet folds, positioned himself and slowly glided inside her. She was so hot. So wet. So tight. It was excruciating pleasure, taking his time, feeling her body adjust and pulsate around him. Once he felt her relax, he eased out slowly only to plunge back in, slowly, then faster, over and over again. For both of them, release came quickly. Ivy dropped to her side. Desmond spooned her, caressed her skin, rubbed her nipples between forefinger and thumb. Soon, he felt her backside push up against him. His sword immediately responded— at attention again. He lifted her leg and started round two. Before the night ended, there'd be a third round. And a fourth. He couldn't get enough of her and had no idea how they'd be able to return to their employer/nanny roles once back in Point du Sable. He had no idea how he'd deal with Shelly. He had no idea how this all would play out.

Desmond and Ivy wrapped up their New York trip with a vegan breakfast of fruit-covered Belgian waffles, a tofu scramble and eggplant bacon before boarding a private plane back home. All was quiet during their return flight. Ivy napped. Desmond thought. He returned to Point du Sable with a game plan. Develop a civil relationship with Shelly. Marry Ivy. He figured everything from there would work itself out. Those decisions made, he allowed himself time to relax and reflect on the weekend. The only thing more surprising than Desiree being left at the guard shack was the past forty-eight hours with Ivy Campbell. He'd unwrapped what he felt was a purposefully nondescript human package to find a loving, funny, passionate, amazing woman inside. And that his mother had set the whole thing up? The one who'd not been overly enthusiastic about any of the society women he'd dated? He knew it was a cliché but truly, wonders never ceased.

Then there was Shelly, and what to do about that situation. He'd called but not gotten an answer. Had texted when she refused to take his call. Kept her updated on what was happening with Desiree and knew that Tami had called her as well. Her only response had been that when he returned to Point du Sable, they needed to talk. She'd remained vague concerning what about and he knew better than to press her. He had a feeling that whatever it was, Shelly wanted to tell him in person. As much as he knew they had to have the conversation, Desmond wasn't even sure that he wanted to know.

He decided to not wait another day for the inevitable confrontation, and texted Shelly as soon as he and Ivy returned to town.

I'm back and would really like to see you. Are you free around seven for dinner at the club?

Her response was immediate. Yep.

Hard to imagine how three letters transmitted attitude but Desmond could have sworn he felt the chill.

Great. I'll reserve a private room.

No. Main dining room. I refuse to be hidden away like a mistress. I'm the mother of your child.

Fair enough. I'll see you soon.

Desmond would have preferred dining in private but when Shelly demanded they eat in the club restaurant, he couldn't think of a way to refuse. Besides serving some of the best food in the country, the main dining room was the place to see and be seen, a point Desmond was sure Shelly took into consideration and why she'd demanded they dine there. Women had always been a rather challenging puzzle and he couldn't put this one together at all. He and Shelly had known each other for years, had always enjoyed a fun, casual, harmless relationship. He partly chalked her acidic demeanor up to being concerned for Desiree, that she perhaps had second thoughts about leaving her as she had. But there was no excuse for how she'd treated Ivy. The rude, possessive woman who'd confronted his nanny wasn't one he wanted to get to know.

Desmond took a quick shower to wash off the fatigue and dressed for the club. He wasn't past using his good looks to his advantage and tonight was no exception. The charcoal brown suit was tailored immaculately, the tan turtleneck worn beneath it complementing his cocoa brown skin. He splashed on a generous amount of a new scent simply called Distinguished, from his favorite designer, Ace Montgomery's latest foray into the world of cologne. Once done, he checked in on Desiree before walking into his multicar garage. He bypassed the Bentley for the less conspicuous but equally exotic Audi R8 sports car in a customized midnight blue. Known for his coolness even when handling billion-dollar transactions, Desmond couldn't lie to himself. He was sweating a meeting he felt was a bit beyond his control. It's why he'd reserved one of the private dining rooms at the upscale club, one that could be reached without notice from a private entrance. The more he thought about it, however, the more he warmed to the idea of meeting in public. He'd have witnesses, which made it less likely Shelly could make up a story to suit whatever she intended. He'd asked for her silence and primary support of her daughter. She may have felt cornered, left without options. There was no telling what a woman who felt desperate might do.

The maître d' greeted him warmly and escorted him to one of their best tables, made partially private by a half wall top with frosted glass.

Desmond wasn't the only one who'd dressed to impress. He'd always found Shelly attractive, had been drawn to how she could be a sophisticate in designer duds one minute and don shorts and a tee and act like one of the boys the next. She'd never shown interest in wanting anything more than the casual relationship they'd enjoyed for years, which was why her secret pregnancy and his subsequent fatherhood was so surprising. Not to mention how she'd treated Ivy. The longer he thought, the more he realized that this could be a long night.

"You're late," was her greeting, though said without much bite.

"My apologies." He reached over and squeezed her shoulder before taking a seat across from her. "I just returned from New York a short while ago. You were my first text."

"Is that supposed to make me feel special?"

"Only informed. Mom says Tami gave you a detailed report regarding Desiree?"

"Yes, and that was totally inappropriate. In fact, the way this entire situation was handled is completely fucked up."

She continued, her tone low and forceful as she leaned in for emphasis, "How dare you make decisions about Desiree without me, then tap one of your employees to be your go-between."

"You were more than welcome to come to New York."

Shelly snorted. "Oh, really?"

"Mom told me you'd decided it best to wait here." Amid her skeptical look, he continued, "No matter what problems may exist between us, I would never keep you from your child."

Shelly shrugged. The sommelier appeared at the table with a bottle of vintage wine. "On the house," he explained, before pouring a tasting. Once Desmond approved, he filled their glasses, gave a slight bow and walked away.

"She's doing much better, by the way."

"Who?"

Desmond's brow creased. "Your daughter."

"Oh." Shelly shifted nervously, and then added, "That's good."

"We were hopeful that the specialists would be able to not only discover her illness but treat it properly. Dr. Kumar is a leading expert in autoimmune deficiencies, especially with children. He believes the disease can be totally eliminated in ten years."

"You said we were hopeful." She put *we* in air quotes.

Damn. The thought that he should have chosen his words more carefully came too late.

"Yes. Mom, Tami…"

"And the nanny, your family's own Cinderella trying to catch the glass slipper…and undoubtedly, the prince."

Flashes of their sensual night together threatened to make a Black man blush. He called upon all of his professional acumen to keep his face neutral and his voice relaxed.

"Ivy was there at the doctor's urging. In her capacity as full-time nanny, she spends more time with the baby than any of us. With all of the other changes happening around Desiree, moving from my home to PDS Medical and then on to New York, not to mention her illness, Dr. Harrison strongly recommended that Ivy accompany her on the plane ride, another first experience and unfamiliar environment for…the child."

Desmond wasn't one to search for words but knew why he hesitated. He had a problem permanently linking himself with Shelly, even in a sentence. He referred to Desiree as his daughter all day long but saying *our daughter* was difficult.

"Ivy was hired because of her stellar credentials. She has a master's in Child Care and Child Management, and is close to receiving a doctorate in Early Education."

"Good for her."

"She takes her job seriously, has excellent skills and loves that baby as though Desiree were her own."

"What about you? How serious are her skills where snagging you are concerned?"

Phenomenal. He shook his head slowly. "I'd think you'd be grateful that…your daughter was receiving that type of care."

Shelly downed her wine and reached for the bottle to refill the glass.

"This bitchiness isn't like you, Shelly. Why do you seem to hate a woman you don't even know?"

"How well do you know her?"

"What's that supposed to mean?"

"It's a straightforward question. How well do you know the woman you trust so much to take care of our daughter?"

"We did an extensive background check. She passed it."

"Did you know she was engaged to Gerald Russell, as in the son of Georgian movers and shakers Gerald Sr. and Bonnie Russell?"

Desmond wasn't sure where Shelly's line of questioning was going, but he was almost positive he didn't want to be along for the ride.

"Yes," was his simple response, though in actuality it wasn't that simple at all. Ivy had never mentioned that Gerald was connected to one of Atlanta's most influential couples. As far as he remembered, she'd never mentioned her fiancé's last name.

"Did you know that he was killed in an automobile accident?"

"Yes, Ivy told me. Did you know her fiancé?"

"No, but I know people who know his family. And from what they told me, your little prima donna isn't all that she appears."

"If we listened to gossip, no one would be as they seemed."

"I heard that—"

"With all due respect, Shelly, I don't care what you heard. My family is satisfied with the care Desiree has been given. Ivy is smart, educated and overqualified for the job that she's taken. Your daughter is lucky to have her. Let's leave it at that."

Shelly shrugged. "Okay, but remember that I tried to warn you. The two of you seemed extra cozy that day I walked into that hospital room. She treated Desiree as though she was the mom. I had her." Shelly stabbed her chest, before taking a calming breath and another sip of wine. "It rubbed me the wrong way."

"Let's talk about that." Knowing they were treading into treacherous emotional waters, he kept his voice calm, almost pleasant. "Why did you decide to have a baby and not tell me? How did you even get pregnant?"

"Well, there's a little dance that happens between an egg and a sperm…"

"You know what I mean. We've been seeing each other for years, almost a decade. I've always used protection. You were on birth control."

"That's correct. I was."

"Then what happened?"

"Can this interrogation wait at least until we've finished the appetizer?"

"Try and see all of this from my perspective. I have so many questions."

"Ones that I will answer, I promise." She looked across the room and gave a casual wave. Desmond turned and saw Brittany, and inwardly moaned. One didn't need a telephone when they had tele-Brittany. He imagined that by tomorrow morning half the town would know he'd had dinner with Shelly and if Brittany caught sight of the waiter delivering their food, an in-depth description of what they'd eaten.

"I understand the Eddington clan is set to expand again soon."

Desmond nodded. "Not soon enough for Cayden. I've seen a few of my classmates and friends excited about fatherhood but Cayden's enthusiasm surprised me."

"What about you, Desmond? How do you feel about being a dad?"

"Initially, I was shell-shocked, as you can probably imagine. Then I was in denial. And after the paternity test—"

"You took a paternity test?"

"Of course. You can't believe I'd simply take your word for a matter that will affect not only me but my family and our lineage for the rest of our lives."

"Well, said like that, of course not."

"After getting the positive results from the test, I was angry, confused. You never talked about marriage or wanting a family. How did two people both using birth control end up with a baby?"

Shelly was quiet a long moment. "At the time, in the moment, I thought it was what I wanted."

"You weren't on birth control?"

"Promise you won't hate me if I tell you the truth?"

Now it was Desmond's turn to pause. "Will you sign

the NDA, so everything that's discussed here tonight remains just between us?" When she remained silent, Desmond began to lose patience. "Shelly, I'm asking nicely. It's the least you could do."

"Fine. But you're damned sure going to buy my silence."

We'll see about that. Desmond hid his true feelings behind a smile. "Thank you."

"I had an operation."

"I don't understand."

"I had a set of eggs surgically removed, and once fertilized with your sperm, the embryo was inserted."

"How? I always used protection. Always!"

"Good grief, Des, with all of your celebrity and athlete friends? You should know better than to leave a used condom at the scene of a casual hookup."

Anger that he didn't know was brewing reached a slow boil. He took a sip of water and was glad for the waiter's interruption. Hearing the suggestions and placing their order gave him enough time to pull himself together.

"You promised not to hate me," she said. For the first time, guilt and remorse showed in her green eyes.

"Your mistake produced Desiree. I could never hate you. But I admit to coming close. For the record, I considered you more than a hookup. I thought we were friends. Worse than planning a baby behind my back, how could you drop her off like junk mail?"

Shelly told him about having second thoughts long after the time for a safe termination. About meeting the banker and being offered the world, along with an ultimatum. No baby. "I had less than forty-eight hours to make a decision. It was a stupid, rash, crazy choice. One I've regretted every day since."

"How are you going to co-parent from way over there?"

"Henry and I aren't married yet. You and I could do it…for the baby."

What Ivy had suggested, but not what Desmond wanted.

"There's way too much water under the bridge for that."

"I figured you'd feel that way. And truth be told, Henry is really the better choice."

Desmond raised a brow.

"He's a good man, very successful. I'm his everything. He adores me. Marrying you would come with a lot of competition, and your mother."

"Careful when talking about my mother."

"I'm just saying…"

"Don't say."

Thankfully, she changed the subject. During dinner, conversation shifted and was pleasant enough. That Shelly didn't bring up Desiree again confirmed that at least for now she was truly not cut out to be a mother. The truth of it left him strangely relieved. When they said goodbye, his hug was brief but genuine. He felt a plethora of emotions driving back home. Mostly, relief.

Shelly agreed to sign the NDA, and to award him sole custody. He agreed to not shut her out of Desiree's life. At the right time, his child would know her birth mother.

He arrived home and after parking, started up the stairway leading directly to the first floor. But looking down the hall and seeing a light shining, he turned and walked toward Ivy's living room. He found her sitting on the couch, her feet beneath her, writing in a planner.

She looked up. Her smile, tentative. "How'd it go?"

"She agreed to sign the papers."

"Desmond, that's great."

"And offered to marry me."

Her face fell.

"That was a joke."

"She didn't ask you?"

"She didn't mean it, Ivy. She was serious about the papers, though. My attorney will draw everything up tomorrow."

"I'm glad everything worked out for you, Desmond."

"She also had news about you." Desmond carefully watched Ivy's response and was pleased when she seemed not to be ruffled.

"What about me?"

"Why didn't you mention that your ex-fiancé was a Russell, a practical dynasty in Atlanta?"

Ivy set down her pen and picked up a glass of sparkling water. "I guess because it never came up. As much as Gerald and I loved each other, his family wasn't keen on our union. Just as I had no desire to navigate their social circles. I always felt they'd come around after Gerald and I married and had children. Now, unfortunately, we'll never know."

"Shelly questioned how well I knew you, basically insinuating that you had something to hide. Don't worry," he continued as he viewed her concerned expression. "I cut her off before she got started. When it comes to helping raise Desiree, you've showed me and my family all that we need to know." He nodded toward the nursery. "How's our princess?"

"Sound asleep."

"What about the full-time nurse you hired? Any problems?"

Ivy shook her head. "Tami's recommendations were spot-on."

"What are you working on?"

"Nothing special." She stood, stretched. "I'm going to bed."

"Want company?"

"I don't think so."

"Telling you about Shelly offering marriage was meant to be funny."

"I'm not laughing."

"I'm sorry." He started toward her. She raised a hand to stop him. "I'm tired, and Desiree will awake in three hours."

"The nurse is here. Why isn't she handling those feedings?"

"Because that's not her job."

He'd so effectively put his foot in his mouth, it's a wonder he made it up the stairs. The relief he'd felt moments ago was replaced with regret at teasing Ivy. He knew she wasn't playful like that. Then he remembered the New York Ivy and made a determination. She needed more fun and less seriousness in her life. He was the man for the job.

Nineteen

She agreed to sign the papers.

And offered to marry me.

Why didn't you mention that your ex-fiancé was a Russell, a practical dynasty in Atlanta?

Shelly questioned how well I knew you, basically insinuating that you had something to hide.

Ivy had tossed and turned all night but woke up to a resolution as bright as the sun. She was going to schedule a visit with Lynn and tender a thirty-day resignation as Desiree's nanny. It wouldn't be easy. She'd signed a contract guaranteeing at least twelve months' employment, with raises and bonuses for each year thereafter. But there had to be a way for her to get out of this, a clause allowing for mental fatigue, physical illness or the pain of mistakenly falling in love with your boss. Shelly's return had forced Ivy to admit what she'd tried to ignore. What was made crystal clear when news of Shelly and Desmond having dinner together had twisted like a knife in her gut. She not only loved Desmond but unlike the warm and tender feelings she'd had for Gerald, she was also in love with him. If being honest, she'd have to admit that since the day that she met him he'd consumed her thoughts and entered her dreams. And unlike the positive outcome that had happened with Desiree, this wasn't an illness a doctor could cure. Only time and distance, not medicine, would help these inappropriate feelings go away. There was no need continuing to mull over it or prolong the inevitable. The longer she stayed, the more attached she'd get to Desiree and the deeper in love she'd fall with Desmond. Better to cut her losses, face whatever happened for breaking her contract and find another job. ASAP. Fortunately, the salary for even this short time was enough for her to secure an apartment and pay rent for a couple months, maybe even put a down payment on a fixer-upper condo. She'd quit, move and figure out life from there. Because staying here any longer than necessary was sure to not end well.

After a quick shower, she pulled on a sweater, jeans and knee-high boots, asked the nurse if she could watch Desiree for a couple hours and then placed a call to Lynn.

"Good morning, Ivy! This is a pleasant surprise."

Until you find out why I'm calling. "Good morning, Lynn."

"How's everything going?"

"Okay."

"Ooh, that doesn't sound too positive. How's your charge?"

That was a loaded question. Navigating this resignation was going to be trickier than Ivy had thought. "She's fine."

Lynn didn't respond.

"Hello? Are you there?"

"You don't have to say anything and don't ask me where

I got the information, but I know that Mona visited the hospital's private wing on a couple occasions and that Desmond was there, too. I also know they called in a pediatric specialist."

Ivy didn't respond.

"It's not my business and I don't want you to go against your NDA, but I didn't know Desmond was listed as the child's father and it's almost impossible for a medical facility to work with anyone except the parent when it comes to a child. Then again, money changes everything and the Eddingtons have influential connections. If anyone can pull off keeping the child a secret while being treated at one of the top hospitals in the country, it's Desmond and his family."

"I can't believe everything you've just told me. If the source was discovered, they'd lose their job."

"And probably their head," Lynn said with a laugh.

"There is nothing funny about this breach of protocol."

"Trust me, the information will go no further. I've been in this business for almost twenty years and have helped raise a slew of Point babies. I know where a lot of skeletons are buried and helped dig some of the graves. People know I can be trusted to keep a confidence. I'm just glad that the baby is doing better."

"Yes, as I said, Desiree is fine."

"What about you, Ivy? How are you doing? Is that stress I hear in your voice or is it just me?"

"You might hear a bit of exhaustion. It's been a busy couple of weeks."

"Try and take advantage of your days off and consider asking to have a few days added to the Memorial Day holiday. It hasn't been a year yet but considering the extra work you've done, they should be okay with giving you a four- or five-day weekend."

"Actually, work and scheduling is why I called. I'd like to come see you today if that's possible. It won't take long."

"It's not something we can discuss by phone?"

"I'd rather not."

"Okay. Hang on a sec." Ivy listened while Lynn punched keys. "My schedule is pretty full today. Are you sure this can't wait until next week? I could take you to lunch then, my treat."

"This won't take long, maybe ten or fifteen minutes. What time should I arrive?"

"You've got me curious, Ivy. Can you make it here in an hour?"

"Absolutely. Thanks, Lynn. I'm on my way."

Thirty minutes later, Ivy sat next to Lynn on a love-seat in her office.

"I know you don't have long, so I'll get right to the point. I'd like to get out of my contract."

Lynn physically reared back. "Whoa! No wonder you didn't want to discuss this while inside his residence. What in the world is going on?"

"A lot, most of which I don't want to get into. I wanted to speak with you before tendering my thirty-day resignation to learn what legal ramifications I could face, and whether there would be a financial cost to leaving now instead of once the year is up."

"I'm sorry, Ivy, but you can't just waltz in here and drop a bomb like that without any explanation. There are always extenuating circumstances that can void almost anything but it has to be something legitimate and the employer, in this case Desmond, would have to agree."

Ivy closed her eyes briefly, then looked straight at Lynn. "I've developed inappropriate feelings for him, Lynn, and can't continue as Desiree's nanny."

"Having the hots for Desmond is what brought you

here?" Lynn chuckled, relaxed and sat back against the cushion. "What woman who's been around him for more than five minutes hasn't fallen in love with that man?"

"This is different. I'm not one easily moved because a man is attractive. It's…everything that's happened, such serious circumstances and so quickly. I've grown attached to Desiree beyond what I feel is…healthy. I don't feel that I can offer the best care given my emotions for her dad."

When Lynn's expression suggested she hadn't been swayed, Ivy took a deep breath and continued, "That's not all."

Lynn sat back. "What more can there be?"

"Gerald's death isn't the only reason I left Atlanta. The other is because of his parents, Gerald Sr. and Bonnie, who blame me for his death."

"I thought you said the two of you were involved in a car accident."

"We were."

"Then how can they blame you?"

"Grief isn't always rational, especially when it involves an only son. I…I convinced Gerald to go out with me that night. I was driving when the other motorist ran the light and practically hit us head-on. The Russells feel that if not for me, their son would still be alive. They spread all kinds of nasty rumors about me, ones that made it impossible for me to stay there and finish my degree. They know a lot of people and have promised to ruin me. After changing my number to cut off future contact, Bonnie located and contacted my mother to try and ascertain my whereabouts."

"That's crazy, Ivy. I'm so sorry to hear you're in this unfortunate situation. I know what happened was not your fault. Surely, you know that, too."

"I do but in this world, perception is reality. The Russells are powerful and very convincing. If the Eddingtons caught wind of what they've been saying, my employment could very well end, anyway. I'm just being proactive before the shoe drops."

"Is it possible you're overreacting? It's not like the Russells are famous. What are the chances that the Eddingtons know them? Even more, because Desiree's existence is being kept secret, what are the chances they'll find out you work for them? Instead of thinking that you need to leave the Estate, that might just be the safest place you can be."

"That's an angle I hadn't considered."

Lynn placed her elbows on the table and leaned toward her. "Please do, Ivy. Because leaving the Eddingtons' employment before your contract expires may not be as easy as you think."

"I understand it might cost me financially. I've saved up most of what I've earned so far so that won't be a problem."

"It's not just that. I negotiated the contract, but Desmond is your employer. It'll be up to him to determine how easy or hard he wants to make your departure. But given everything he's been through with his daughter and the unique nature of the whole situation I can't imagine he'll be happy with the idea of a stranger coming in to replace you.

"You're already months into the contract. Maybe by the time it's up, this will have all blown over. A year goes by quickly. To not honor the contract could lead to not only financial implications, but legal ones as well."

The visit ended with Ivy promising to keep Lynn posted. Ivy asked Lynn to search her records for a possible replacement, just in case. She thought of stopping by her mother's house but a check of her watch showed she'd already been gone for over an hour. She was still on the clock, so to speak. Time to get back home and wait for Desmond. She didn't want to spend another sleepless night without having followed through on her plans.

Once back home, she changed and fed Desiree, cleaned up the nursery and tried to busy herself with other mind-numbing chores. Her heart felt heavy, but Ivy refused to feel bad. Desiree's condition had been diagnosed and was being treated. New York was magical. Making love to Desmond had been nothing short of amazing, easily the best sex she'd ever had in her life. None of this changed Ivy's decision. It just made it harder. Next to burying Gerald, leaving that beautiful baby girl and her magnetic father would be the hardest thing she'd have to do in life. And that was only if she could convince Desmond to let her out of the contract Lynn assured her was ironclad. She had to make a sound case. He had to see reason. Remaining in the house of the man she'd now fallen even deeper in love with was totally not an option.

"Good evening, Ivy Campbell, best nanny that money can buy."

Deep in thought, Ivy hadn't heard Desmond enter the suite's living room. "Hey, Desmond."

He entered, smiling. "How's everything going?"

"Desiree's good. Dr. Harrison came by and checked on her. Said she was doing well enough for the nurse to go home for the evening."

"I can't believe how much she's improved since they formulated the right treatment plan."

"Babies are resilient."

"And amazing." He leaned down and placed a kiss near the top of her head. "Don't go anywhere. I'll be right back." Desmond left and went to check on his daughter. It took everything in Ivy to not get up and pace the room.

"I need to share something with you," she blurted out, while one of his feet was in the room and the other one still in the hallway.

He stopped, legs spread and with hands on hips. "Don't tell me. You're pregnant."

"No!"

"Whew!" Desmond smiled. His eyes teased and twinkled. "Just kidding, Ivy. Though honestly, I couldn't handle another round of news like that right now."

"You used protection, remember?"

"Not that last night, if you'll remember. Anyway, I also used protection the night Desiree was conceived."

"She's one of the two-percenters?"

"No, she's one of the less-than-a-quarter percent whose mother stole the father's sperm and injected it into her body."

Ivy gasped. "You can't be serious."

"I lie not."

She forgot all about her impending announcement and crossed back over to where he sat. She took a seat on the short side of the L-shaped sofa.

"Shelly…"

"Waited until I fell asleep and then retrieved my used condom."

"I've heard of that happening."

"Yeah, so had I. Just didn't think it was something I'd ever experience from the women I allowed in my life."

"Why do you think she did it?"

"She offered me a long and convoluted explanation but the short of it was to trap me."

"But she abandoned the baby."

"Once Desiree was a reality, she realized that she didn't really want to be a mother and was in over her head. The reality of the baby's impending birth and a timely romantic opportunity further confirmed it."

Ivy listened as Desmond recounted what Shelly had shared, becoming more incredulous by each passing word.

"But why not come and tell you all of this before having the baby? Why did she dump off Desiree like an internet order?"

"The guy agreed to help her if she gave up the baby. She did and they moved to Fiji where she's been living in the lap of luxury with her retired bank exec."

"But when she heard about Desiree's illness, she cared enough to come back. That has to mean something."

"I believe she loves Desiree. I also believe that my requesting the NDA and sole custody led her to revisit her decisions, and wonder if the choices she'd made were the correct ones."

"She suggested the two of you get married."

"I believe a part of her wondered if there was any chance that she and I could make a go of it and raise Desiree together. A part of me feels that was somewhat out of obligation, as though she should at least make the offer to be a part of raising her child. I would never prevent her and Desi from having a relationship, but my trust in her is irretrievably broken. We'll maintain a friendship for the sake of our daughter but that's all it will ever be, platonic friends, nothing more."

Ivy didn't realize she was holding her breath while waiting for the answer until it came out in a soft whoosh of relief. The timing was definitely off for a resignation, given the news that he'd just shared. Desmond scooted over and pulled her into his arms, making rational thought nearly impossible.

"Now, what is it you wanted to share with me?"

Ivy tried to swallow her fear and dredge up the courage to tell Desmond about the Russells. But maybe it wasn't necessary. Maybe Lynn was right, that this storm would pass over and the year would go by without having to share her secret. She needed this job until she could secure another. She'd start checking out employment opportunities right away but for now, she needed to work.

"Just, um, an update on your daughter. I've been monitoring her temperature and behavior closely. It's as if she never was sick."

"We have you largely to thank for that. Your acute observations helped in treating her quickly. How can I ever repay you for all you've done?"

Let me out of my contract? "It's just part of my job."

Ivy watched Desmond close the difference between them. It took every ounce of discipline not to run away. Even so, she stiffened as his arms came around her.

After a brief hug, he eyed her closely.

"Are you okay?"

"I will be. A good night's sleep will help."

"Then I'll leave you to it." He leaned over and placed a kiss on her forehead. Ivy couldn't help but inhale his manly scent. It was almost enough to undo her, to make her reach out and pull him into the bedroom, have him make love to her throughout the night, the way they'd done in New York. Instead, she walked to the door and sent a clear message.

Opening it, she told him, "Good night."

Twenty

Desmond wasn't sure how or when it happened, but Ivy had managed to do what no other woman had. Get under his skin and crawl into his heart. He wasn't yet ready to use the *L* word. But there was a way he felt about her that hadn't quite happened with anyone else. Even after her actions, there was a deep affection for Shelly. Even though she'd yet to sign the legal documents, he didn't hate her. Thanks to his mother's wisdom, he understood. A few of his model/actress friends had turned him out in the bedroom and taken him on an emotional whirl. But this feeling was different, deeper, harder to define. With Ivy, it wasn't the attributes that normally attracted him, such as a beautiful body, similar interests or mutual friends. It was the way she held Desiree, the attention she showed his daughter. It was her thoughtfulness, her kindness, the slow burning sexual fire that once unleashed was hot enough to consume them both. Again, he wasn't ready to admit any of this. Even closed up in his home office as he was, consid-

ering marriage, he told himself it was strictly business, a
way to lessen any potential scandal Desiree's unexpected
and as-yet-unannounced appearance may cause. Derrick
had just gained a huge endorsement from one of the Society's highest members, the vice president of the United
States. His father's campaign success was all but decided.
He'd become the next president of the Society of Ma'at.
After that, the sky was the limit and who knew? Derrick
might enter politics and follow in the VP's footsteps. He'd
tossed the idea around for years now and had only backed
away from a bid for Illinois senator when another charis-
matic, well-heeled brother had thrown his hat in the ring.
That man served only one term as senator before making
the leap to the world's highest office. With the connections
a Society presidency afforded him, Derrick could bypass
state politics if he wanted, and go straight for the brass ring.

A knock on the door jolted him out of his musings.
"It's open."

He was surprised to look up and see Derrick entering
the room. "Dad! What are you doing here?"

"Damn, son. I know it doesn't happen often. But is it
really that shocking for me to visit from time to time?"

"Of course not. I was just thinking about you, that's all.
Right before you knocked on the door."

"Do I want to hear what about?" Derrick asked.

"About you becoming president."

"Ah. Of the Society?"

Derrick shook his head. "Of the United States."

A slow smile spread across Derrick's handsome face.
"Someone raised you right."

"Sure did. Her name is Mona."

"Arrogant asshole."

"Chip off the old block."

The two men shared another laugh. Desmond relaxed

into the comforting presence of the man who was not only his father but also a confidant and best friend.

"So does that mean Shelly has signed the papers?"

"Not yet but she has them. I expect them back shortly."

"Are you sure you can trust her to keep silent?"

"I'll never fully understand why Shelly did what she did, but I don't believe she's vindictive. Our friendship goes back almost to childhood and our families know each other. She understands how important reputation and social standing is in this community. A scandal for us would equally hurt her family. She won't say anything."

"For her sake, I hope that's true."

Desmond felt a drop in the room's temperature. When it came to his empire, much like Mona, Derrick Eddington didn't play games.

"How's the presidency campaign going? Another few months and you'll be on the top of the mountain."

"I felt that way until an hour ago."

"What happened an hour ago?"

"A call from Bob." Derrick sighed as he ran a hand over his face. "Looks like we've got a situation."

Every nerve in Desmond's body stood at attention. "Involving Desiree?"

"And the nanny."

"Ivy? How is she involved?"

"The fiancé she told us about during the interview, the one killed in a car accident?"

"Gerald Russell."

"Right. The only son of a brother."

"Oh no, Dad. I didn't know he was Society. And the only son...wow." Desmond stood and walked to the window. A few seconds passed before he turned and said, "What does that accident, as unfortunate as it is, have to do with your confirmation as president?"

"Ivy was driving at the time of the accident. The Russells blame her for their son's death."

Desmond returned to his desk and sat down heavily. He wracked his brain to remember their past conversations and couldn't find one where she'd told him who was driving.

"I'm pretty sure Ivy told me it was raining that night, and someone ran a light."

"Bob didn't know what information the parents have that make them so adamant about their accusation. Whatever they've got was enough for them to hire a law firm to try and sue her for negligent homicide."

"Ivy's been to court?"

Derrick shook his head. "There wasn't enough evidence for the case to go to trial, but Bonnie, Gerald's mother, vowed to keep fighting. It appears she created a hot enough fire for Ivy to drop out of school and leave town, which only gave Bonnie even more reason to keep pursuing what she feels to be justice for her son. So much so that she hired a private detective to track down Ivy."

"No effing way."

"Ivy's mother lives in Chicago. Her place was put under surveillance. A while back, Ivy was seen going into said residence holding a baby's car seat. When she left, the detective trailed her back to Point du Sable."

"And to the Estate."

"Exactly."

"But they couldn't get any farther than the guard's gate. Ivy could have been coming here for any number of reasons. For all Gerald's parents know, the baby is hers."

"A twenty-five-thousand-dollar payout told them otherwise."

"Sarge talked?"

"No, but someone did. Unfortunately, with as many people as we employ, it could be anybody—security, housekeeping, landscaping, someone doing repair. Even with an NDA, that kind of money can open up the most trusted mouth. And even if we questioned everyone and forced lie detector tests, there's no guarantee we'd ever learn the truth."

"So…Bob and the committee know I have a child?"

"I told Bob the truth, felt I had to. He promised to keep a lid on it for now."

"That's a good thing, right?"

"That's only part of the problem. Gerald Sr. went to the committee with his version of the truth—that the woman who killed his only son is employed by our family. Even unproven, that puts me in a bad light, made even worse by the fact that Bob grilled me about anything that could bring on scrutiny and I swore to him that he had nothing to worry about."

"You were telling the truth, Dad. You couldn't have known this would come up. None of us did."

Desmond eyed his dad for a long moment, his heart breaking at the weary look in Derrick's eyes.

"What are we going to do? What do you want me to do?"

"Talk to Ivy, get her side. Maybe things will look brighter from a more balanced perspective."

"You've got it," Desmond replied, reaching for his phone.

Derrick stood and headed toward the door. "Let me know what you find out."

"Most definitely," Desmond replied, with a resolute nod.

His mind raced as he punched in Ivy's number, hoping that she had an explanation that made sense. If what the Russells said was true, that would make her a liar. The only thing worse than a liar was a thief, and if his father's bid for presidency was lost as a result of her dishonesty, well, she might as well be called that, too.

Twenty-One

Desmond was just about to tap Ivy's number when he decided on another approach and called his assistant instead.

"Hey, Jan. Do I have any appointments for the rest of the day?"

"Um, don't think so." He listened to her humming off-key, and chuckled. "No, Desmond. Nothing until tomorrow's luncheon at the Chamber of Commerce."

"I'm going to cut this one short and head out early. If you've finished everything that's time-sensitive, feel free to take off, too."

"Thanks, sir! Someone is sure in a good mood these days."

He'd known Janice for most of his life and felt bad that for her Desiree was still a secret. He really needed to figure out the proper way to announce her presence in the family to the public. He was too proud of a papa to keep her hidden much longer. After having been faced with the prospect of losing her, and with her so much better, he was ready to let the world know about his baby girl. And more importantly, he wanted to be the one to announce it. He didn't want Desiree to be rolled out like a tabloid story, on the lips of all of high society in Point du Sable.

He left the office and headed home. On the way there, he rang the staff phone at his parents' estate.

"Good afternoon, Eddington residence. How may I direct your call?"

"Chauncey, it's Desmond. Where's your wife?"

"Conducting a staff meeting with housekeeping. Do you need her?"

"I was hoping she could come down and watch Desiree this evening. The nurse will be there, too. There's a quick trip I need to make. I want Ivy to come with me."

"How soon do you need her?"

"As soon as she finishes whatever is going on now."

"Consider it handled, Desmond. I'll let her know."

Not wanting to let on that anything was amiss, Desmond forced a smile into his voice. He scrolled to Ivy's name on his directory and tapped her number.

"Hey, Desmond, what's up?"

"What are you wearing?"

"Excuse me?"

"Ha! I thought that question would catch you off guard. Throw on some jeans, sneakers and a heavy jacket. I've left work and am swinging by to get you. We need to take a little trip."

"Where?"

"Don't worry about that. Just be ready."

"Desmond, I can't. The baby—"

"Will be well taken care of. Bernice is on her way down. The sooner we get off the phone, the faster you can get ready. Remember, dress comfortably. I'll see you in ten."

When Desmond arrived, Ivy wasn't smiling, but she was ready. Bernice arrived shortly after him.

"Where are we going?" Ivy asked him. "What's this about?"

"Something that I think you will like. Do you trust me?"

Ivy looked skeptical. "I don't know."

"Fair enough. Let's go."

His Audi sports coupe was the perfect vehicle to cover a lot of highway quickly. He reached the private airstrip in no time. The plane was waiting, and running, the pilot on the tarmac talking with one of the ground crew.

"Desmond," Ivy drew out his name. "Where are we going?"

"Someplace fun." He pulled into a nearby parking space and killed the engine. "Come on."

Placing a hand at the small of her back, Desmond led Ivy to the plane and up the airstair. After introducing her to the pilot and both meeting the attendant who would handle this flight, he stepped back and allowed Ivy to enter before him. She took two steps and stopped cold.

"Wow."

"Nice, huh."

"I can't believe this is a plane. It looks nothing like the one we boarded taking Desiree to New York."

"This is part of the Eddington Enterprise fleet."

"You have more than one?"

"A few." He grabbed her hand and kissed it. "I'll give you a tour. It will take all of five minutes."

The first section of the customized Airbus 380 resembled a living room, with curved benched seating covered in soft cream leather and textured walls with accents in black, silver and gold. The floor was a hardwood ebony. A bamboo runner ran the length of the plane. The next section housed a rectangular dining table with seating for eight.

"This serves as a boardroom in the daytime and formal dining at night," Desmond explained, as Ivy looked around, still in mild disbelief. "That wall is actually a projection screen."

With the push of a button, the ceiling opened and a fifty-two inch curved LCD screen unfolded.

"The plane is wired for surround sound, the chairs as well for those wanting an immersion experience. With the right action movie or ones made in 3D, the experience is especially cool."

The pilot walked toward them. "We'll be taking off in about five minutes, sir. If that's alright with you."

"That's perfect."

Desmond finished with a quick walk-through of the plane's fully functional kitchen with wine cooler, full-sized marble bath with a state-of-the-art power shower, and a luxury bedroom with a queen-plus-sized bed covered in plush linen and pillows, interactive smart screens built into the wall and modern light fixtures throughout for that extra touch of chic. They returned to their seats and the plane took off, soaring above Chicago, Lake Michigan and heading north.

The attendant came out with two flutes of champagne. "Thought you might like these to kick off your journey."

"I knew that I liked you," Desmond teased, taking the flutes and passing one to Ivy. "To the best nanny anywhere, period. And the only woman I can see looking after my daughter. I appreciate you, Ivy.

"The last trip was all about my baby and work. This one is all about fun."

He tipped his glass to clink hers.

"I would have been impressed with a thank-you card but, hey…"

Desmond almost spewed out his drink.

"Seriously, I can't believe people really live like this. I mean, of course, I've heard of private planes before, but this is a house."

"It's definitely top-tier but our company makes no apology for the money we spend. Our executives travel a lot and all over the world. Flights can last upward of twenty-four hours if traveling nonstop, with business meetings having to take place at odd hours, depending on the destination. It's important that we arrive ready to work. A plane like this allows us to do that."

"A plane like this should almost do the work for you."

"Cayden is the techie in the company. I'm sure he's working on it."

With the champagne halfway gone, Ivy finally relaxed. She leaned against him. "Can you tell me where we're going now?"

"Minneapolis."

"Hmm. What's there?"

"A museum I've been wanting to visit."

"That sounds interesting. What kind of museum?"

"Ever hear of a guy named Prince?"

The private two-hour guided tour was fabulous. When Ivy squealed while being allowed to touch one of the artist's guitars, Desmond knew his trip idea was money. A few dead presidents gave the guide incentive to open the gift shop. They came out loaded down with bags filled with memorabilia—hats, jackets, jewelry, albums, even a Paisley Park tambourine. The gourmet meal of glazed salmon served over toasted pearl couscous was as good as what would be served at a restaurant bearing a Michelin star. They'd had a ball in Minneapolis. On the return flight to Chicago, Desmond wanted nothing more than to close the privacy door between them and the crew and end their excursion on a sexual note. But instead of pleasure, it was time for business. While drinking their after-dinner coffees, he dove into the real reason for the trip.

"Tell me again why you left Atlanta." He felt Ivy's eyes on his and forced his face and body to remain neutral.

"I guess for several reasons, but the main one was the accident that killed my fiancé."

"What were some of the other reasons?"

"Desmond, what is this about?"

He shrugged. "Getting personal. I know Ivy the nanny. I want to get to know Ivy the woman."

Ivy settled back and looked out the window. "Everything in the city reminded me of Gerald and our time together. The accident occurred not far from where we lived. I had to drive past that spot every day."

"I can't imagine the type of pain you were in that made you leave school so close to getting your doctorate."

"With Gerald gone, Atlanta didn't feel like home anymore."

"What about his family? They had to have been supportive, considering what all you went through."

Ivy remained silent.

"Weren't they?"

"Gerald's family never really liked me. I think they had someone else in mind for their son. Someone more…sophisticated. A prettier, more polished type who'd grown up and traveled in the same circles that he did."

"And after the accident?"

"We went our separate ways."

Desmond's mood slipped. He'd given Ivy every opportunity to come clean. Clearly, she didn't intend to tell him the truth. If she was lying about this, what else could be a falsehood? Was she really a doctoral student? What was her real connection to Lynn, his friend's wife? Had she used their friendship to gain entry into his household?

All of the doubts felt from their initial interview came roaring back.

"Just like that, huh?"

"It wasn't that simple, but I really don't want to talk about it."

"Unfortunately, Ivy, that topic you haven't wanted to talk about is the main one we should have discussed."

Twenty-Two

Ivy went on red alert. Something was wrong. Something had shifted. A night that could have been pulled from any woman's fantasy book seemed to be going to hell in a handbasket. What could have happened to change the mood? There was only one way to find out. Ivy shifted so that she looked directly at Desmond.

"Is there something specific you want to ask me?"

"Yes. I want to know why you're lying right now to my face?" His voice was calm but his eyes shot daggers.

"Lying about what?"

"Everything. The accident. Gerald's parents. Why you left Atlanta."

Ivy swallowed, her heart sinking further with every word said. She looked away from Desmond. "I didn't lie to you," she said softly. "I may not have revealed everything, but I didn't lie."

"Did you cause the accident?"

Her head whipped around. "No!"

Desmond's eyes narrowed.

"Would you like to see the police report? It proves that the other driver was at fault."

"I don't have to see the report to know that's true. Again, not because of what you're telling me, but because when Gerald's parents tried to sue you for negligence, there wasn't enough evidence to make a case."

Ivy's eyes conveyed her shock.

"Was that what you didn't want to discuss, Ivy? How you were embroiled in a criminal investigation involving Gerald Russell Sr., one of Atlanta's most prominent citizens?"

"How did you find out?" Ivy could barely hear the question over the rapid beat of her heart.

"One of the members of the Society on the committee to elect their next president is a friend of the family and contacted us to warn us about this potential threat to his campaign."

"I'm sorry that I didn't tell you, Desmond, but it wasn't an attempt to be blatantly untruthful. It was because I wanted to put the past behind me. Gerald's parents are hurting and lashed out in their grief, accusing me of causing the accident when deep down they know that's not true. The police report and witness accounts bear that out. It's why the case never went to trial and why I didn't feel the need to bring it up.

"But I still don't understand why whoever this person was that spoke with your father knew about me. Outside of Lynn and my mother, no one knows who I work for or where I am. And only Lynn knows that I work for you, specifically. My mom knows I'm a nanny at the Estate but I purposely kept the details general. I could be working for anyone, including someone not related to your family."

Desmond took a deep breath. He spoke to her while looking out the window.

"Your mother's house has been under surveillance. You went there one day, with Desiree. A detective saw you walk in with the car seat. When you left, you were followed to our house. Even without access past the gate, your comings and goings revealed enough for the Russells to know that you were connected to my family.

"Bottom line, you lied to me."

"Desmond, I—"

"When asked directly if there was anything not found during the background check that we needed to know, you said that there wasn't."

"I didn't think you needed to know about that."

"You were wrong!"

"None of what the Russells are saying is true!"

"Still, your omission gave us a false representation. You aren't the person you told us you were."

"I am exactly that person."

"My family values loyalty and trust above all else. It's possible that you're loyal. But you can't be trusted."

"What exactly are you saying?"

"I'm saying that your services are no longer needed. Once home, you'll have twenty-four hours to gather up the necessities you'll need for the night. I'll have a company pack up the rest of your things and deliver them to whatever address you provide."

"Desmond, please…"

"I've made my decision. It's not up for discussion. You had a chance to come clean and you continued to lie." He stood and looked down on her. "That action told me what I needed to know."

Desmond stormed down the aisle into the bedroom and closed the door. He never came out. Back in Chicago, there were two cars waiting at the airport. She got into one of the waiting town cars and was driven back to the Estate. Once there, still in shock she worked quickly, on autopilot. The next twenty-four hours went by in a fog. Ivy threw a few articles of clothing and all her toiletries into a suitcase. She pulled out the matching carry-on and placed her tablet and important paperwork inside. Unable to bear hearing her mother's criticism, she found a short-term furnished condo rental online. Twelve hours after one of her best dates ever, Ivy was in her car—basically homeless and definitely jobless—heading to Chicago and the uncertain future that awaited her there.

She held it together long enough to retrieve the key and garage key card from the lockbox, park her car and lug her luggage inside. She stripped and stepped into the shower. Only then, under the spray of a rainfall showerhead, did she let her tears join the water that fell. She cried for herself, and for Desiree. It wasn't fair that Desmond hadn't given her a chance to say goodbye. Sure, the child wasn't yet a year old but babies had feelings. She'd wonder where Ivy had gone. Once out of the shower, her sadness turned to anger. How dare the Russells have her followed. How dare they continue maligning her name. It was horrible what happened to their son, but it wasn't fair that they try and ruin her life.

Finally, with somewhere to channel her anger and direct her focus, she picked up the phone only to quickly put it down again. Who in the heck was she going to call that could go up against the Russells? They'd been powerful enough to run her out of town, and were rich enough to afford the best lawyers, ones that could undoubtedly run rings around those she could afford. Wearing an oversized tee from the Prince museum, Ivy paced the floor, wracking her brain. How could she put an end to this bullying?

How could she stop this cloud of sorrow from raining on the rest of her life?

Ivy stopped suddenly as a name came to mind. She rushed over to her phone and tapped a number before she could overthink the decision and change her mind.

"Mona, it's Ivy. Please don't hang up. I'll understand if after today you never want to see or speak to me again, but please, one hour, that's all I ask. I want someone in your family to hear me out, and to know the truth."

Later that afternoon, there was a knock on the condo door. Ivy, having pulled on a pair of black leggings to complement the purple-and-black tee, took a deep breath, said a quick prayer and walked to the door. She looked through the peephole and gasped.

Jerking open the door, she exclaimed, "Desiree!"

With tear-filled eyes, she looked at Mona. "Thanks for bringing her. I didn't get to say goodbye."

"I know you didn't."

"Please come in."

Ivy took the car seat from Mona and motioned toward the living room. "Please, have a seat."

"Wow, you move fast."

"I had to. Desmond gave me twenty-four hours to leave his employ. It's a short-term rental." Ivy followed Mona into the living room. She sat on the opposite end of the couch and pulled Desiree from her car seat. "Hello, my sweet angel. Hi, Desiree!"

She spoke and played with Desiree for a bit, then sat the baby against the back of the couch and placed a throw pillow in front of her.

"I assume you know what happened."

"Derrick told me about the Russells and their accusations."

"That's what they are, Mona, accusations, not facts. I

have the police report to prove that I never lied to Desmond. The Russells never approved of me and now blame me for their son's death. I know it's out of grief but it's still not right. Bonnie vowed to basically make my life a living hell, and that's exactly what she's doing."

"Why didn't you share this with us, being one-hundred percent forthcoming with what was going on?"

As she had with Desmond, Ivy explained how she felt she'd put the past behind her. "I considered the slate clean," she finished, "and saw no reason to bring up someone else's vendetta. I wasn't trying to hide anything. I didn't mean to lie. I was as forthcoming as I felt I needed to be about everything I thought mattered. The police report clearly shows that I'm not guilty of Gerald's parents' accusations. The case was thrown out. That's why I didn't say anything. In my mind, there was nothing to share."

A long pause and then, "I believe you."

Ivy was stunned. "You...you do?"

"The Russells aren't the only ones who can hire an investigator. I've decided to do a little digging myself."

"You have?"

"Yes, and he's not going to leave one stone regarding that family unturned. Meanwhile, I have several friends in Atlanta. One, a former college classmate, grew up with Bonnie, your late fiancé's mother. From what I learned, she's the last one who should threaten to ruin someone's life."

"Why do you say that?"

"Let's just say, she has secrets that she doesn't want her husband to know. One involves his best friend and a close encounter of the extramarital kind."

Ivy was shocked. "No."

Mona examined her manicure and wedding rings. "Now, I'm not one to gossip but let me say this. If the

Russells try and mess with me and mine, including sabotaging Derrick's nomination or exposing what they think they might know about my son and a baby? I'll give them all that they can handle, and then some."

Mona's visit was short, supporting Ivy's rationale while making it clear she'd back whatever decision Desmond made. Ivy understood. For the next few days, she tried to put back the pieces of her life. She researched doctoral programs in Chicago, as well as the chances of completing hers online. She had lunch with Lynn and told her what happened. Thankfully, with the money she'd saved, there was no need to rush into another job. She also visited her mom and while not divulging that she no longer worked for the Eddingtons, she did share her plans to finish her degree and to one day open a school for girls. About a week after leaving Desmond's house, she returned from the complex gym to the shock of a lifetime—Desmond, at her front door.

"What are you doing here?"

"May I come in?"

"Okay." Ivy's hands shook as she placed her key in the lock. She walked in, allowed Desmond to enter, then closed the door behind him.

"What do you want?"

"To talk to you. May I have a seat?"

"What you have to say will take that long?"

Desmond stepped back and leaned against the door. "I'm sorry."

Ivy crossed her arms. "You talked to your mother."

"Yes, and Dad. And Bob Masters, one of Dad's sponsors. And the investigator that Mom hired."

"And?"

"I was wrong to have fired you."

"It took all of those people to tell you that?"

"Yes." He walked into her living room and sat in a chair. "Will you allow me to explain?"

"The same way you allowed me to explain my situation to you?"

"I should have listened."

Ivy walked over to the couch and sat down. "I'm listening."

"This year, I endured the ultimate betrayal. A woman used nefarious means to get pregnant with my child, had said child without telling me and then had her delivered to my house via courier. Shelly is someone I've known practically my whole life, someone I trusted. The worst thing ever was having her lie to me."

"And then you felt that I did the same thing." Ivy spoke softly, and without judgment. She could actually see Desmond's point of view.

"It's one of the reasons I grilled you that night. Because I didn't want any secrets between me and whoever lived in my house. I didn't want any more *gotcha* surprises out of the blue. Even more, I didn't want to be the reason my father wasn't elected Society president. So when my father came to the office with what he'd learned, that not only was Gerald Russell a brother but your late fiancé's grieving dad, one who wanted to ruin you, I believed that in the process of doing that they could bring down my family as well."

"I'm sorry."

"I know."

"What happens now? With your father?"

"He's still in the review process."

"What happens if the Russells try and go against him? I'll feel horribly if your knowing me somehow impacts his chances."

"I don't think we have to worry about that."

Ivy searched Desmond's face. His slight impish smile confused her.

"Mom took a trip to Atlanta."

"Really?"

"She had lunch with Bonnie."

"Oh." Ivy felt nauseous. She wrung her hands. "How'd that go?"

"As well as can be expected, given the circumstances. They came to an understanding. Bonnie agreed that it was time for her to move on with the rest of her life and leave you alone."

"I can't believe that will ever happen."

"They won't come after you again, Ivy. You have my word."

Ivy's relief shot her out of the chair and into Desmond's arms. "Thank you!" she cried, with tears flowing. "I couldn't fight them, had no idea how I'd ever get my life back."

Realizing her actions, she pulled back and wiped her eyes. "Thank you. I don't know what I'll ever do to pay you back."

"You can help me clear the last potential hurdle to my father being elected. My status as a single dad."

"Anything," Ivy said sincerely.

"Great. Will you marry me?"

Ivy stepped back, as though physically punched.

"Absolutely…not."

Twenty-Three

It was not the answer Desmond had expected.

"Why not?" he queried once an eternity passed.

"I'll help out in any way other than that, Desmond, but when it comes to getting married as a business arrangement, I have to say no."

"We haven't even discussed the offer. Not in detail."

"Yes, we did. Four million dollars in exchange for five of my childbearing years in exchange for school funding. Is that about right?"

"Well, yeah, but not quite like that."

"What is it quite like, Desmond? How would you like me to pretty up this business transaction? Call it a marriage of mock motherhood, maybe? A marriage for motives of utmost respect?"

She returned to the chair and plopped down. "I can't do it."

Desmond rubbed the stubble on his chin. "Do you think marriage to me would be that bad?"

"You're talking about this as though you're talking about going to the movies or choosing a rental car or buying a house. I know that these days marriage is valued less than the paper the license is printed on. And the practical side of me knows that I'm being a fool. But…"

"But what?"

"But I'm… It's just that…I'm falling in love with you, okay? There. I said it."

"Seriously?"

"Maybe right now it's more like I lust you. Or deeply like you. Either way it's close enough for jazz."

His laugh was soft and sexy. He walked over and pulled her up and into his arms. Something long and growing increasingly hard suggested he lusted her, too.

"What you're feeling is more emotion than in some marriages I know."

Once again, she twisted to face him. "What about you?"

"What about me?"

"Can you say that you're falling in love with me? That you're feeling something deeper than an employer/employee connection."

"I can say that my feelings for you are intense. I can say that besides Desiree, there's no other female in my life. You're smart and beautiful, and Desiree adores you."

"So you're fond of me because I'm a good nanny."

"And a great lover," he said, sliding his hands down to cup her ass. "Don't forget that."

She stilled the hand inching high toward the vee in her thighs. "Desmond, this is ridiculous."

"What?"

"This is not how people get married. Maybe it is for some, but not me. Marrying you in exchange for money, even for my dream of a girl's school, feels… It doesn't feel right."

"But you just said you're not marrying me for money. You're marrying me for l-l-l-l-lust."

"It's not funny," she said, trying hard not to laugh. "I don't even know you. Not really."

"I'm getting to know you well enough."

"Let's find out. Where was I born?"

"Chicago."

"Wrong. Gary, Indiana."

"Close enough for jazz," he said, playfully mocking her earlier tone. "When's your birthday?"

"March twenty-seventh."

"Why didn't you tell me? We could have celebrated."

She shrugged. "We never made a big deal of them in my house. Not unless it was a major one. Thirteen, sixteen, twenty-one. When is yours?"

"December sixteenth."

"A Sagittarius. I should have known."

"What does that mean? Or do I want to know?"

"I haven't known many but for the most part you guys are cool."

"Glad to hear, not that I'm much into all that. What's your sign?"

"Ha! The one you're not into? I'm an Aries."

"Is that a good thing?"

"The best."

"I'll be the judge of that." He pressed his lips to hers— once, twice, a third time.

"What's my favorite color?" Ivy asked.

"Um, blue? No, purple!"

"That one was easy."

He reached for her hand and walked them back over to the couch. Once there, they sat down with his arm around her.

"Ask me my favorite color?"

She entwined her leg with his. "What's your favorite color?"

"Ivy."

She gave a playful punch. "You're lying."

"That's the truth, baby. I've always loved the color green."

"I don't think I can have just a fling with you."

"I'm not asking you to."

They talked well into the night, learning more about each other. Ivy was surprised by some of what she learned. Mona's humble beginnings with her father, a one-man CPA firm, and her mother, a homemaker. How selling the business after he retired provided the start-up money for Derrick's grand plans. And how for the first few years of their marriage, Mona had been the breadwinner, putting her business degree to good use until Eddington Enterprise turned a clear profit. She admired, even envied the family's closeness, and that they had an extended family with whom they were close as well.

They made love slowly, leisurely, studying each other's body like a research assignment until they both passed the class. A little before six o'clock, Ivy felt Desmond ease out of bed, kiss her forehead, whisper his goodbyes and leave the condo. She turned over, fluffed the pillow, and tried to sleep for another hour. But turning down Desmond's proposal, such as it was, became increasingly uncomfortable.

Finally, she gave up, sat up and tossed a pillow at the wall.

"Ivy, what the heck have you done?"

Twenty-Four

"She turned me down."

It was a little after seven o'clock. Desmond was in Jake's office enjoying a strong and much-needed cup of Joe. With two shots of espresso. His lethargic body suggested that he needed two more.

"Get the hell outta here. Are you serious?"

"Called it marrying for money."

"How much money?"

"Four million dollars to start her school, and additional funding for at least ten years thereafter."

"Damn, she's a real one."

"What do you mean?"

"Dude, I know women who'd marry me for five thousand dollars, let alone four mil. That's the kind of woman you want in your life. One who doesn't want a man for his money, but for who he is."

Desmond flopped back against the leather chair. "Whose side are you on?"

"Yours, bro."

"Shelly signed the papers. The lawyer's bringing them by later today."

"There's good news."

Desmond nodded, took another sip and winced at the brew's strength. "Still need to figure out how to announce Desiree's arrival. She's growing bigger every day. We can't hide her forever."

"Or have someone else break the news. You know this town. And with her hospital stay? Believe me, there are more people than we know who have the news already."

"What do you suggest? That I send out press releases or go live on Facebook?"

"It's about as personal as asking a woman to marry you for cold hard cash."

"I confided in Aaron Rutherford about it."

"Who's that?"

"The president of Trinity Children's Hospital."

"He's Society?"

Desmond nodded.

"Well, I'll be damned. Small world."

"He didn't think the news would be as big a deal as we're making it."

"Not with our generation but with Dad's and the men older than him. They're old-school men with traditional values."

"Whose voices hold sway over a huge voting bloc."

"Would it be better to break the news now or if Dad gets elected?"

"You meant when he gets elected, right?"

"Yeah. When."

Jake stood and walked from one side of the room to the other. "I think it would be best to break the news after convincing Ivy to be your real wife."

* * *

Jake's sarcastic comment sent Desmond on a mission. For the next couple months, they officially dated. He invited Ivy to social events, introduced her to friends. His sister Maeve included her in some of their social outings, a silent nod that she approved of his choice. Avery had her baby, a boy. Cayden was ecstatic. When they had a family dinner to celebrate, Desmond brought Ivy. Ivy brought Desiree. Shelly returned to Fiji. Rumor had it, she'd gotten engaged.

June was their first real break from each other. Desmond was traveling in the luxurious company *house plane* as Ivy called it. Sydney, Ghana, Senegal, Tanzania—he was out of the country for almost a month. When he returned, Desiree began to crawl toward him. And then… the little princess got up and walked! Something so small yet so major brought more joy than Desmond could have imagined. It was as though his daughter waited until he got back to take her first steps.

In ways big and small, Desmond showed Ivy how he felt about her, that she was more than an employee, not just a nanny to his child. She spent time in his spacious master suite, but not as much as he wanted. "The baby," she'd remind him when he tried to convince her to stay there. Even with the high-end monitor with a video screen, Ivy wasn't comfortable being a floor away.

On the Fourth of July, there was a picnic on the grounds of the country club. Desmond encouraged Ivy to invite Helen. Ivy didn't speak much about her mother, her only close family.

"When you marry a woman, you marry her family," his mother informed him. "Best to know we'll all get along."

By September, it was clear. Ivy was an amazing woman, definitely marriage material. Someone worthy of a proposal felt from the heart. But was he really ready to make that leap? Desmond wasn't sure. Eddington men were faithful, another part of their legacy. His parents had been married for thirty-three years without one extramarital affair between them.

"Be sure before slipping on that ring," his paternal grandfather had told him on more than one occasion. "When you take a wife, she's the only one for life, so make sure you love what you're getting."

At the end of September, just before the annual meeting for the Society of Ma'at, Derrick and Desmond had dinner at the club. Just the two of them.

"I talked to the elders," Derrick explained, using the title given to those fraternity members aged seventy-five plus. "Told them about your situation."

"They want to talk to you for one thing. You're going before council."

"Dad! We still had time to handle this before the election." Desmond was nervous immediately. "Are you sure that was wise?"

"I want to enter that election with integrity. There can be no secrets between brothers."

"Ah, man." Desmond hung his head a bit, then raised his eyes to look at his father. "What else did they say?"

"They told me to tell you congratulations. They know that being a single father isn't easy, and that you're a good man."

When dinner ended, father and son shared a hearty embrace. That night, Desmond felt the weight of the world falling off his shoulders. He wasn't yet totally out of the woods. There was still the matter of Point du Sable's group of gossipers ready to snap up the latest news and spread their embellished take on it around town. Whatever happened now, he thought he could deal with it. He had the support of his brothers.

If he had any sense, a little voice whispered inside him, he'd have Ivy, too.

Twenty-Five

An alarm woke Ivy before 5:00 a.m. Not from the clock on her bedside table or the one on her cell phone. This signal came from deep within her, from the depths of her soul. It vibrated within her blood cells and rocked her foundation with the strength of its truth. She'd fallen in love with Desmond Eddington. It was a fact she'd run from since the day of their first kiss, but one that could no longer be denied. She loved him, and no matter the fear and trepidation, the insecurities and potential drama, the possibility of sadness and disappointment that went with the self-proclaimed declaration, Ivy was ready to embrace this truth and officially step into a life far beyond her wildest imaginations. Neither her favorite soothing classical music nor attempts at meditation could lull her back to sleep, so after almost an hour of tossing and turning, she climbed out of bed and headed for the kitchen and a cup of tea that may soothe where sleep did not. There was a lot to think about. Mona warned her during their first meeting that seemed a lifetime ago.

With Desmond, you'll need both, encased in skin thick enough to withstand Lake Michigan. Naked. In the dead of winter... He may come off uncaring or brusque, but inside that armor beats a very big heart.

After a bathroom pit stop, Ivy continued down the hall and up the stairs to the gourmet kitchen that now felt like a second home. She pulled down Mona's favorite tea that she, too, now loved and brewed a pot of steamy goodness simply dressed with vanilla almond creamer. Afterward, she bypassed the marble countertop bar and continued to the downstairs living room outside her suite, one of her favorite rooms in Desmond's massive house. The sun shone bright against a cloudless sky. Foliage—thick, vibrant, abundant—surrounded the near floor-to-ceiling windows, adding its beauty to the large potted plants inside. A gurgling fountain flowed into the multilevel koi pond, restocked once summer had solidified its presence with brightly colored koi, goldfish and exotic shubunkins, which was the centerpiece of the garden just outside the room. Ivy walked to the window, sipped her tea and allowed the acknowledgment of her love for Desmond, the love she'd denied for so very long, to spill out of her soul and into the atmosphere. To crystallize into a reality that lived outside her body. The truth settled around her shoulders like a scratchy sweater—warm and wanted, even needed perhaps, but ill-fitting and uncomfortable. A year ago, she would not have allowed herself to admit these feelings. But the past five months changed everything. Desmond hadn't used the *L* word and told her he loved her. But his family choosing her dream as the foundation's first focus next year was beyond anything she could have imagined. And undoubtedly Desmond's idea. The school for girls would be Point du Sable's first private educational institution and would offer hope and possibility to young bright minds. Marrying him and making a family for Desiree, even one of convenience, was the least she could do.

For the first time since Gerald died, Ivy was ready to face the issues that had prevented her from living life to its full potential. A new life was at her fingertips. It was time to let go of the past so that she could embrace the future. The thought filled her with apprehension and excitement. She couldn't wait to see Desmond, wanted to tell him her decision before she chickened out and changed her mind.

She called him. "Hey, what time do you think you'll be home?"

"I've still got a bunch unchecked on my to-do list. At least a couple hours."

Ivy couldn't wait that long. "Do you mind if I come by real quick?"

"What's going on? Is it Desiree?"

"No, the baby is fine. I have something to tell you that's rather important. I don't want to share it over the phone." When he remained silent, she added, "I promise, this won't take long."

Fortunately, Mona was home and agreed to watch Desiree. Ivy jumped in her Kia and went to the building that Eddington Enterprise built. She'd passed it dozens of times but this was her first time inside. It was a modern architectural wonder of granite, steel and burnished maple. Ivy saw none of it, only the elevator that would take her to Desmond's office on one of the top floors.

He met her in the lobby.

"Thanks for agreeing to see me," she said, sounding breathless.

"You said it was important."

"It is."

"Come on back to my office."

The silence unnerved her as they entered the massive space.

"I'll marry you," she told him as soon as he closed the door.

"Come again?"

"I said I wouldn't change my mind but that was then and this is now and you're funding my school. I mean your family's foundation but still, I know it was your idea."

"Do you love me?"

Ivy loved him and was in love with him, but did she want to admit it? He'd still never expressed a similar feeling, which meant that as much fun as they'd had and as attentive as he'd been, this might still be just another business project, his past actions all part of closing the deal.

"I really like you," she teased, trying to lighten the moment. "I adore your daughter. I respect your family and would be honored to help preserve the Eddington name. So, that said, will you marry me?"

Desmond peered at her, his face like stone, his body stance like that of a warrior as he answered, "Absolutely not."

Twenty-Six

A week later, Desmond sat in the corner booth of a swanky restaurant on Chicago's famed Gold Coast, waiting for Ivy and talking with Maeve.

"I don't like him, not for you."

"Thanks for the opinion that I didn't ask for, big brother. I think we're about twenty years from the days you could tell me what to do."

"Could I ever?" He looked up and saw Ivy walking toward him. "Ivy's here, sis. Have fun in Mexico."

"Give Ivy my regards." He stood, drinking in the woman who'd opened up a part of himself he hadn't known was closed, who'd quietly and without his conscious knowing tipped her way into his heart. Tonight, she looked especially lovely, a vibrant blue dress complementing bronzed skin and a toned body no longer hidden inside bulky clothing. Tonight, the hair always pulled into a ponytail or topknot when she first began caring for Desi boasted big loose curls that tumbled over her shoulders. Hers wasn't the overt sexuality that turned every man's head when she walked into the room. Ivy's was an almost hidden sensuality, a heat smoldering below a placid demeanor of serious contemplation, a woman focused on the task at hand, paying attention to others instead of herself.

She reached the table and accepted his brief warm embrace as he whispered into her ear, "You look amazing."

"Thank you." She sat opposite him, setting down her purse as she looked around. "I'd never heard of this place before. It's so…upscale, almost too much for what's supposed to be a simple dinner."

"I don't remember using the word *simple* in the text that I sent you."

"No, you didn't. I assumed…"

"You know what they say about that word." Desmond sat back, smiling. "What did you think tonight was about?"

Ivy shrugged. "I don't know. A date, of sorts?"

"Of sorts."

The maître d' stopped at their table. After welcoming them, he waved over the sommelier, who recommended a robust pinot noir that would pair well with their appetizer choices of roasted bone marrow with parsley and brown butter brioche, and a Caesar salad of wood-fired romaine, pecorino and savory sprinkles over a soft-cooked egg.

Ivy watched the sommelier's stiff-backed exit. "I've never eaten bone marrow."

"You're in for a treat."

"I'll trust you."

"I like the sound of that."

Ivy's comment was regarding his starter suggestion, but Desmond hoped that in time that perspective would cover much more.

"How was my daughter when you left her?"

"About to be spoiled rotten by her doting grandparents."

"I have no doubt."

"Please try and talk Mona out of what she's planning for Desi's birthday. I know they're excited and this is her first one but her ideas are over-the-top, completely too much."

"Is *completely too much* even a grammatical possibility?"

"Only with the Eddingtons."

The smile in Desmond's heart spread to his face. "You're delightful, do you know that?"

"I don't think that's ever been a word to describe me."

"I'm glad to be the first to let you know."

They continued eating. "Wait, did I forget your birthday?"

He shook his head. "December, remember?"

"Right, the sixteenth. I'm just trying to figure out what's the special occasion."

"Does it have to be anything special for me to invite you to dinner?"

"To a place like this with food this good? Yes."

She finished a bite and wiped her mouth with a napkin. "I know! It's one of the companies you flew out in June to meet with. You closed a huge mega-trillion deal."

"Not quite, but from your lips to their ears."

Dessert arrived, a culinary masterpiece. Flames danced around the cone-shaped slice of chocolate cake with caramel "lava" as the waiter set it on the table. The fire died out. Ivy noticed something else blue and large and sparkly in the middle. She picked up her fork to remove what she thought to be an edible crystal-like substance much like edible gold.

It wasn't a crystal.

It wasn't edible.

Her mouth dropped open as her incredulous eyes slowly

rose to meet Desmond's near-laughing ones. He gently pulled the ring off the fork still poised in midair. "Once before I asked a question, but learned it wasn't how proposals were done."

He slid out of the booth and onto one knee. "So, I thought I'd try it again. I love you, Ivy Campbell. Will you do the honor of being my wife?"

Cheers from the surrounding tables drowned out her answer. She leaned down and spoke into Desmond's ear.

"Absolutely."

Twenty-Seven

A year later...

A group of one hundred diamond-dripping, designer-clad guests mixed and mingled in the Eddingtons' solarium and on the patio outside. The sun was glowing, the breeze was gentle, the temperature hovered at sixty-five degrees. Strategically placed heaters kept those who needed them warm outside, while a blue-tinged fire contrasting against white lava rocks in the solarium's custom fireplace provided a cozy upscale atmosphere for those enjoying Mona's exotic garden. Male gloved waiters offered flutes of Dom's Plenitude Brut Rose and Krug Clos d'Ambonnay while their female counterparts presented Beluga caviar and crème fraîche tartlets, bacon-wrapped lobster, Breedlove beef barbecue sliders and white truffle and couscous-stuffed mushrooms dipped in gold leaf. A combination of white wooden benches and white folding chairs with padded seating were connected with strips of gray and purple silk. Rows of organza formed a tent and billowed softly overhead. A quintet played a combination of classic soul instrumentals, smooth jazz and neo-soul, catering to the variety of generations in attendance. The biggest hint of the special occasion was a floral archway of white and purple orchids, hydrangea and moonflowers at the entrance of the glass bridge over a koi pond. Tinkling laughter and subdued conversation mingled with the early evening air. Cayden Barker and his wife, Avery, were chatting with Lynn and her ex-Pro Bowl guy when he glanced at his watch. He whispered to Avery, then crossed the room, nodded at the houseman keeping watch at the door and entered the sanctity of the Eddington Estate.

Taking the steps of the home's double staircase two at a time, he went down a couple halls before reaching a room on the home's north wing and tapping on the door.

Desmond sat in a professional barber's chair where an attendant perfectly lined his close-cropped coils. "Enter at your own risk."

"So you are still here," Cayden responded once inside the suite. "I thought that perhaps you'd gotten cold feet and escaped the crowd in the back by bolting out the front door."

"Naw, man, I'm not going anywhere."

"Are you sure? Last chance before the ball and chain gets placed around your ankle."

Jake rounded the corner, looking debonair in a charcoal gray tux. "Don't give the brother any crazy ideas. It's almost showtime."

"That's why I came up. Do you need anything, Desmond? Cologne? Lotion? A shot of whiskey?"

"Man, get out of here with that. I wasn't at all nervous until you walked into the room."

"You've got to be nervous. It's required of the groom."

Jake looked at his watch. "We probably should head on out."

As if on cue, Mona tapped on the door and stuck her head in. "Showtime, fellas. Jake, Maeve is already at the altar. As soon as you're in place, we can begin."

Jake strolled down the center aisle. He gave Maeve a hug before they both turned toward the entrance. The quintet eased into a sweet instrumental of one of the couple's favorite songs by Prince.

"Adore."

Ivy stepped out of the shadows and stood beside Desmond. He looked dashing, his gray tux complete with tails. Ivy was resplendent in a mermaid-styled masterpiece of silk, satin and lace, the romantic vee neckline spotlighting a five-carat teardrop diamond Desmond had gifted her the night before. Together, they walked down the aisle to where the pastor stood, with eyes only for each other. Their custom vows included words from the song playing, with no mention or hint of a business transaction. The ceremony was short and sweet, but touching.

"Desmond, you may kiss your bride."

Oohs and aahs accompanied the extended lip-lock. The couple laughed and hugged. Ivy wiped away tears. Bernice came down the aisle carrying Desiree, an angel draped in folds of white lace and sporting white satin booties, and deposited her into Desmond's arms.

"And now ladies and gentlemen, it is my pleasure to introduce to you Mr. and Mrs. Desmond Eddington, and their daughter, Desiree."

The crowd applauded. The party began. And so, too, did the rest of their lives.

* * * * *

WE HOPE YOU ENJOYED THIS BOOK FROM

HARLEQUIN
DESIRE

*Luxury, scandal, desire—welcome to
the lives of the American elite.*

Be transported to the worlds of oil barons, family dynasties,
moguls and celebrities. Get ready for juicy plot twists,
delicious sensuality and intriguing scandal.

6 NEW BOOKS AVAILABLE EVERY MONTH!

#2893 VACATION CRUSH
Texas Cattleman's Club: Ranchers and Rivals
by Yahrah St. John
What do you do after confessing a crush on an accidental livestream? Take a vacation to escape the gossip! But when Natalie Hastings gets to the resort, her crush—handsome rancher Jonathan Lattimore—is there too. Will one little vacation fling be enough?

#2894 THE MARRIAGE MANDATE
Dynasties: Tech Tycoons • by Shannon McKenna
Pressured into marrying, heiress Maddie Moss chooses the last man in the world her family will accept—her brother's ex–business partner, Jack Daly. Accused of destroying the company, Jack can use the opportunity to finally prove his innocence—but only if he can resist Maddie...

#2895 A RANCHER'S REWARD
Heirs of Hardwell Ranch • by J. Margot Critch
To earn a large inheritance, playboy rancher Garrett Hardwell needs a fake fiancée—fast! Wedding planner Willa Statler is the best choice. The problem? She's his best friend's younger sister! With so much at stake, will their very real connection ruin everything?

#2896 SECOND CHANCE VOWS
Angel's Share • by Jules Bennett
Despite their undeniable chemistry, Camden Preston and Delilah Hawthorn are separating. With divorce looming, Delilah is shocked when her blind date at a masquerade gala turns out to be her husband! The attraction's still there, but can they overcome what tore them apart?

#2897 BLACK SHEEP BARGAIN
Billionaires of Boston • by Naima Simone
Abandoned at birth, CEO Nico Morgan will upend the one thing his father loved most—his company. Integral to the plan is a charming partner, and that's his ex, Athena Evans. But old feelings and hot passion could derail everything...

#2898 SECRET LIVED AFTER HOURS
The Kane Heirs • by Cynthia St. Aubin
Finding his father's assistant at an underground fight club, playboy Mason Kane realizes he isn't the only one leading a double life. So he offers Charlotte Westbrook a whirlwind Riviera fling to help her loosen up, but it could cost her job and her heart...

HDCNM0722

SPECIAL EXCERPT FROM

(H)HARLEQUIN

DESIRE

*Home due to tragedy, exes Felicity Vance and
Wynn Oliver don't expect to see one another, but Wynn
needs a caregiver for the baby niece now entrusted in
his care. But when one hot night changes everything,
will secrets from their past ruin it all?*

Read on for a sneak peek at
The Comeback Heir
by USA TODAY *bestselling author Janice Maynard*

"This won't work. You know it won't." Felicity
continued. "If the baby is your priority, then you and
I can't…"

Can't what?" Wynn smiled mockingly.

"You're taunting me, but I don't know why."

"You don't want to *enjoy* each other while you're
here?"

"We had our chance. We didn't make it work. And
I'm not one for fooling around just for a few orgasms."

"The old Fliss never said things like that."

"The old *Felicity* was an eighteen-year-old kid."

"You always seemed mature for your age. You had
a vision for your future and you made it happen. I'm
proud of you."

She gaped at him. "Thank you."

"I'm sorry," he said gruffly. "I shouldn't have kissed you. Let's pretend it never happened. A fresh start, Fliss. Please?"

"Of course. We're both here to honor Shandy and care for her daughter. I don't think we should do anything to mess that up."

"Agreed."

Don't miss what happens next in...
The Comeback Heir
by USA TODAY *bestselling author Janice Maynard.*

Available September 2022 wherever
Harlequin Desire books and ebooks are sold.

Harlequin.com

Get 4 FREE REWARDS!

We'll send you 2 FREE Books **plus** 2 FREE Mystery Gifts.

FREE Value Over **$20**

Both the **Harlequin® Desire** and **Harlequin Presents®** series feature compelling novels filled with passion, sensuality and intriguing scandals.